FATE OF THE LYING JADE

In Spain, some twenty years after the war, Blake is trying to rescue a wayward daughter from trouble and return her to her politician father. But, after being trapped and shot at in a deserted village, with Blake in hot pursuit, the girl escapes to an equally deserted mine. There, exploration reveals a hoard of Nazi tat, including hideous busts and pornographic monstrosities. When diamonds are found hidden in the busts, the Germans and the Spanish converge on the mine to claim them. But then there is what appears to be an earthquake . . .

Fate of the lying jade

ROTA

Charges are payable on books overdue at public libraries. This book is
due for return by the last date shown but if not required by another
reader may be renewed - ask at the library, telephone or write quoting
the last date and the details shown above.

JOHN NEWTON CHANCE

FATE OF THE LYING JADE

Complete and Unabridged

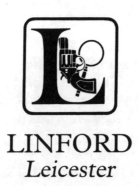

LINFORD
Leicester

First published in Great Britain in 1968 by
Robert Hale Limited
London

First Linford Edition
published 2005
by arrangement with
Robert Hale Limited
London

British Library CIP Data

Chance, John Newton
  Fate of the lying jade.—Large print ed.—
Linford mystery library
  1. Detective and mystery stories
  2. Large type books
  I. Title
  823.9'14 [F]

  ISBN 1–84395–786–8

Published by
F. A. Thorpe (Publishing)
Anstey, Leicestershire

Set by Words & Graphics Ltd.
Anstey, Leicestershire
Printed and bound in Great Britain by
T. J. International Ltd., Padstow, Cornwall

This book is printed on acid-free paper

1

I think the Spanish invented siesta owing to the extreme heat of their summer afternoons. The shadows on the dirty white houses are all dead black under the eaves and lintels. The sky is as blue as a Technicolor scene for Don Quixote. The wind doesn't bother to move. It is siesta there, too.

The shutters over the windows were broken, the slats crooked and some missing altogether. Through this lopsided grille I watched the dusty village street.

The once white walls of the houses were patched where the finish had broken away. The red pantiles on the roofs were often toothless, and in some places the rafters showed in big patches where the tiles had slipped off altogether. Windows were matt black where there was any glass left and the shutters hung drunkenly. The dusty road and the patios were scattered with broken, fallen roof tiles and chimneys, bits that had slowly fallen off the houses.

A scene of desolation, silent, forgotten. Except, of course, for the two of us.

She was a fine girl, very dark, so that there was a deep blue light in her hair which matched her eyes. They were big, sometimes helpless, sometimes innocent, sometimes mischievous, sometimes downright naughty. She wore a pair of large ear-rings, concentric gold rings, the inner one turning inside the bigger; gyroscopes. At the moment she wore a torn shirt that strained to hold her rich young bosom inside, riding breeches and one cheek was streaked with dirt.

She smiled at me, and handed me a reloaded revolver.

'Do you think we'll get out alive?' she said.

I left the street to itself for a while and smiled back.

'An interesting question,' I said. 'What I ought to know before I guess an answer is, what have you been doing that somebody wants to kill you?'

The eyes were big and innocent.

'But nothing — nothing at all!' She shook her head and the ear-rings jangled.

2

'I can't imagine why they're doing this!'

I sighed and looked out at the deserted street. Somewhere there were four men, hiding, having failed at the first attempt to shoot us out of this empty house.

The last we had seen was a solitary man standing at the middle of the road, a rifle in his hand, bawling up at our window in a Portuguese-American accent.

'Come on out with your hands up, else you'll come out with your feet up.'

In the houses behind him there were three more men, I knew, with their guns trained on our house, but they were well hidden. All that had been twenty minutes ago. We had heard a car go off from somewhere down the street. My car was still hidden in the stables at the back.

The men had not gone round there for our window commanded the only way through to the back. Behind that was a rock cliff which reached out arms either side of our house, like the headlands of a bay.

'Wouldn't it be a good idea to run for it while they're gone?' she said.

'We don't know where they've gone.

And you surely don't think they've all gone?'

'I don't know. I've never been laid siege to before.'

'I'm surprised at that,' I said.

She laughed, then lit two cigarettes and gave me one.

'There's a kiss on it,' she said.

'What a time,' I said, and put my left arm round her and kissed her properly. Then I looked out of the window again. 'I don't know why I'm doing this. You could kiss your way out of anything.'

'It was nice of you to come,' she said and a shifting change from innocence to naughtiness shone in her eyes.

'I did this for your father,' I said. 'He was very kind to me once. 'Would you please go to Spain and fetch my daughter back', he said. 'She's in trouble there'. Do you know what I thought he meant by trouble? Arrested for bathing in the nude. I didn't bargain for this sort of do.'

The silence outside remained unbroken. It was beginning to look as if the besiegers had gone. Perhaps they meant it to look like that.

I sat down on a broken chair, the gun resting on my knee. She came and leant on my shoulder and looked out.

'What did you steal?' I said. 'You'll have to let me know in the end.'

'Nothing, nothing, darling, nothing,' she said, but she touched her open shirt with a hand as if to make sure something was still there.

I'd have got it out there and then, but it would be too risky to start a struggle and shift our attention from the window.

The peace outside continued.

'Who are these men? You must know some of them?'

'I know Ferdi. That's the one who came and shouted out there. I met him in a night club at Santander, but I didn't know he was a crook.'

'Perhaps he didn't know you were.'

'You're being just nasty.'

'I have a right to be. I come here to fetch you because your Daddy's broken his leg. I get to the hotel and you run out pursued by gunmen. I get you into my car and we race off without any time for explanation.

'They chase us. We go like the bats of hell, doubling, sliding, screaming and then take this turn to mislead them only to find the damn place is a dead end. And here we are, being shot at. What for? Why should I die when I landed only this morning?'

'It's one of those things that happen here,' she said. 'They chase single girls in Spain, you know.'

'You don't mean these fellows just want to pinch your bottom, do you? Do you think I'm cracked or something? You've done something bloody. What it is I don't know, but it's dead bad. Why? Your father's got plenty of dough. Why do you have to steal?'

'If I took anything at all,' she said, a little haughtily, 'it was mine. I'm not a thief.'

'Why wouldn't you let me drive to the police, then? What was all that panic when I suggested it?'

'They're so awful, these Spanish police. They just put you in prison for weeks and weeks and nobody can do anything about it.'

6

'Not if you haven't done anything.'

'Oh yes they do. They put you in and then try and find out what you have done. They're terribly unfair.'

We were quiet for some minutes because we could hear a car in the distance, perhaps down on the main road, for the noise faded away and the silence came again.

It was very hot, and the strain of watching the sunburnt desolation made my eyes gritty.

'Funny there's nobody here,' she said, staring out.

'A mining village, probably,' I said. 'But if you had time to notice when we came in, instead of looking backwards all the time, you'll see the cliff fell on half the village. That's why the road doesn't go on and why we've got an arc of cliff behind us, which is why I ducked in here.'

'An avalanche, you mean?'

'I think that's the technical term for when half a mountain falls on you.'

'I suppose no more's going to fall?' she said, big eyed.

'That is the least of our troubles right

7

now. One at a time.'

The horrid silence came again.

'I wonder if they did go?' she said.

'There's a couple of old hats out in the hall and a broom. Get one and the broom.'

She did. It was a very old dodge, but one which nearly always worked because only a bullet could tell whether there was a head in the hat.

I pushed the shutter open a bit, and then shoved the hat out on the broom-handle, turning it slightly as if somebody under the brim was looking up and down the remains of the street.

The shot came from a house on our left across the road. It went through the hat and ripped a foot of wood slat from the other shutter.

I pulled the hat back and closed the shutter again.

'That ground floor window, left and two along,' I said.

'What nasty people,' she said, sticking her finger through the hole in the hat.

'What do you know about this Ferdi?'

'He dances in a very rude way,' she

8

said. 'I had to pinch him very hard to stop him.'

'You shouldn't be out alone,' I said. 'Do you know anything about him?'

'He followed me around. I thought it was natural until all this happened.'

'When did you dance?'

'Last night.'

'He came up to your table and asked you?'

'That's the way it happens. Then when I'd pinched him we sat down and he turned on charm galore and bought wine. I had a hard job to get into my room and shut the door in time. Fancy him being a bloody crook!'

'Yes. Fancy. Well, what happened this morning?'

'I took a little ride. Then when I went back one of these men was in my room, turning it upside down. I ran out through the windows before he could get hold of me. In fact, he tripped on the bedclothes he'd pulled off the bed. I got over the balcony and down the vine, then I ran through the gardens and saw the others coming from the back way. Then I saw you, my hero, I love you.'

'So I should think,' I said. 'One part you left out.'

'What, darling?'

'How you happen to be running around with a thirty-eight stuck down your riding boot or wherever you had it and a pocket full of spare ammo.'

'I stuck it in my belt under my shirt. I couldn't get it in my boot, you fool. It would bulge madly. As it was it felt jolly cold and uncomfortable.'

'A comforting discomfort. But you didn't say why.'

'A girl needs protection. After last night and Ferdi, I mean.'

'Why are you such a little liar as well as a thief? What the blazes are you up to? Come to that, what am I up to, and what for?'

'Because you're a darling hero, and I love you.'

Then she grabbed my face and started kissing it all over. I shoved her off. She was laughing breathlessly.

'Don't block the view,' I said.

The silence went on. I had seen a

smoke puff from that window drift away up in the hot air, and that was all that had moved in half an hour.

Another shot came across the street and hit the wall by our window. Plaster broke off, fell and smashed in the courtyard. A puff of smoke came out of a window to the right of us and up on the first floor of a house half wrecked by fallen rock.

'A reminder, or fixer,' I said. 'They couldn't have seen us in here.'

'Why don't they shoot all the time?' she said petulantly. 'It's much better than waiting and not knowing where they are.'

'They could be moving about over there,' I said, 'there are four joining houses on our left, one and a half on our right and a lot of stables and general litter six foot high dead opposite.'

'Look. Why don't we make a run for it?' she said, as if suggesting we might go for a bathe or have tea.

'It was bad enough coming here when they were a half-mile behind us, and still got my windscreen twice. They'll do much better from just across the road.'

11

'You're nothing but a depressant,' she said, and pouted. 'I can't bear doing nothing.'

'It will be a change for you, I'd guess,' I said.

The silence came again.

'How is Daddy?'

I couldn't help laughing. She was such a beautiful scatterbrain.

'I said he had a broken leg.'

'How?'

'I don't know.' In fact he'd told me. 'Fell out of Tilly's bed. Don't spread it.' Tilly being his secretary at the Ministry it was for me unspreadable. How he and she had dressed, got that leg out, down in the lift, into her car and back to the steps of his house is beyond me, too. A Spartan, for he hadn't yelled till the sound of that car had gone twenty minutes.

Small wonder his daughter was careless of pain. Hers and anybody else's.

He had called his daughter Flip Side because he had expected a boy. In some respects, he'd got one.

'Is it all right now?'

'It's in fair condition for a broken leg. Why do you think he didn't come himself?'

'I didn't really think,' she said, staring out of the window. 'Everything's been such a rush today.'

'Great fish!' I said. 'I wish you understood the language. Or even just anything.'

★ ★ ★

I had known her father for many years but his daughter for only two. I had met her first without knowing who her father was; a simple contrivance with this girl, for she never told the truth any time I could remember. Not viciously, but because it was more fun making things up.

There wasn't all that much difference, I suppose, between a politician who lies for a living and his daughter who lies for fun. Anyhow, the quixotic business of carting the broken leg away to pretend he'd done it on his own doorstep was only a lie, anyhow.

'Have you got something on you that you can just chuck out of the window and buy them off?' I said.

She shook her head and the ear-rings spun like goldfish bowls.

'Oh, no,' she said. 'Nothing like that.'

'Well, an idea hits me,' I said. 'One or two men have gone. The remaining men are firing to keep us in here. So why? This is an old mining district. There could be jelly about in the workings or the work huts. Suppose they come back and threaten to blow this place up? Do you fancy that?'

'Don't be silly! They wouldn't dare!'

'They've been trying to kill us for quite a while. What else wouldn't they dare? Do use a little sense.'

'Can't we get out the back way and climb the rock?'

'What's left looks about three hundred feet, overhanging.'

She went out. I heard her soft sandals shiffing through the dust of the rooms. She was having a look for herself.

I kept cursing myself for not having driven direct to the police, but calmer

14

thought — and there was a lot of time for that now — showed we should never have made it.

In the city with the traffic and blocks and holdups we should have been shot through in no time. It was the more or less open road, superior speed and a lot of luck which had got us this far. And this far wasn't enviable, but we were still whole.

She came back, sulky, so I didn't ask what she hadn't found.

'Tell me what you hid with the gun,' I said. 'Open up now. If I've got to share your punishment, I ought to know why. What have you got in your shirt?'

'Mr. Blake!' she said, and laughed.

'Don't fool about. What is it? What did you steal?'

'I didn't steal anything. I keep telling you!'

'What did you borrow?'

'Nothing.'

'I'm getting mad,' I said. 'Very, very wild.'

She came over to me and put an arm round my neck.

15

'I bought something,' she said, making it sound as if it meant nothing at all.

'Well knowing it to have been stolen?'

'The girl said, 'Buy this from me', and I gave her the money and took it.'

'What is it?'

'Just a little map.'

'What did you pay?'

'A hundred pounds.'

'Did you know the girl?'

'Of course I knew the girl! You don't think I'd give that money to strangers, do you?'

'Well, who was it?'

'The girl I came over to see.'

'I thought the girl was just a figment, without which your father would have blocked your coming.'

'Well, that's where you're just wrong. Stella was here all right, and in some trouble. She had to have this money.'

'Why?'

'Look! A car!'

She was at my right side and could see slantingly through the shutters down to the end of the street. I stood up and went close to her.

16

At the end of the street a dusty blue Peugeot was on the point of stopping from a crawl. It was about a hundred yards away and had obviously rolled down the gradient to where it was now, for we had heard nothing.

The doors opened like an elephant's ears. I held the gun ready, but it was too far off to get a shot.

Two men got out and stood looking towards us. One was Ferdi. The other I didn't know, but I hadn't had time to get to know anybody but Ferdi.

'Is that one of them?' I said.

She squinted a little covering the distance.

'I think it's the man who stripped my room.'

'You knew what was going to happen, didn't you?'

'You never know in Spain.'

'Where did you get the gun? Stella?'

'Yes. Ten pounds.'

'Quite a handy girl, isn't she?'

'She knows people.'

'I suppose she's got a gun, too? Or didn't she need it after she'd sold you the map?'

'I don't know.' She had her chin on my shoulder. 'What are they doing?'

'Talking, by the look of it.'

They were talking, but they kept looking down the street towards our hideout. It was very obvious something was going to happen before long, and it would be a big throw, designed to get us out of the house with our hands up.

I hadn't been serious about gelignite. That would have blown us apart and the map, too.

'What will they do?' she said.

'Don't guess, wait. I think the idea is to get us out as whole as possible, and get rid of us later.'

'You didn't say that before.'

'The conference up the road indicates there is no great hurry for a little while. If they'd meant to blast us they wouldn't wait, I think.'

'Perhaps they're trying to shake us out by doing nothing,' she said, and sounded tense.

'That would take too long. Be patient . . . What did Ferdi talk about?'

'Me. You know these foreigners.'

'And you told him all about yourself?'

'I told him my father was a goldsmith and my mother held the main share in Jacobson and Gilt, the diamond merchants in Hatton Garden.'

'That was insensible of you. Why tell a yarn like that?'

'I just thought of it.'

'I bet.'

The men at the car looked down towards us again, then the bedroom stripper threw down a cigarette and heeled it into the dust. It was getting hotter than ever.

Ferdi was talking, and with the gestures of his hands and shoulders I guessed it was some specific instructions he was giving.

'You don't think you've lied yourself into a kidnap?' I said.

'Goodness! I hadn't thought of that.'

'Because it isn't true. But it could give a line. Show me the map.'

She hesitated. I kept my eyes down on the conference on the road but grabbed her arm and shook it.

'Come on! Bring it out!'

She brought out a small roll of paper, big and thin as a pencil stub.

'Unroll it.'

She fumbled. That and the tenseness of her voice were the only signs I had seen that she was inwardly shaken.

I glanced down. River, a hill, spotty blocks of scattered buildings. It could have been a bit of anywhere, and it had no title.

'Okay. Put it back. Do you know what it means?'

The show up the road had stopped again. Both men were looking down towards our house.

'Treasure,' she said.

'Oh, for heaven's sake, not that,' I said. 'Shovel that back in with your goldsmith father and diamond-studded mother.'

'Well, it is,' she hissed. 'Why do you think I paid all that money?'

'How did you get all that money? Your father said you had only enough to last a week, which at your rate of output would probably mean a couple of days.'

'I just had it,' she said. 'What are they doing?'

'Nothing.'

But then Ferdi raised a hand like a bidder at an auction. He kept it there, his head turned, still looking down the street under his white hat. The hand dropped again. Nothing happened.

'He was signalling to the men across the road,' I said. 'Any minute, now, I guess.'

Yet still they hung on. I was beginning to feel rattled myself, though it was not the first time I had been in such situations. I have lived not a very honest life in the past.

It occurred to me then to wonder if her father had used his knowledge of this to instigate this excursion to fetch his daughter.

'Does your father know about this map?' I said.

'Oh, don't be silly,' she said. 'How could he?'

'There are telephones.'

'Oh, so there are,' she said airily. 'I hadn't thought of that. But isn't he in hospital or something?'

'No. He's at home.'

We didn't say anything for a minute or more because the bedroom stripper had got into the car. But Ferdi remained standing by it and the doors remained as before, elephant's ears.

'Perhaps they're waiting for tea,' she said, and giggled.

I kept glancing across the windows to the mentally marked windows but saw nothing of the men there, nor at any other windows either.

'Go back a bit. You bought this map last night?'

'Yesterday afternoon, really, it was. She won't go out after dark for the time being.'

'Why? Is she on probation? Under a government curfew?'

'I don't know her business.'

'She must have told you why she wanted the money. Or did you know what you were buying?'

'Of course I knew. All that money — '

'You didn't say where you'd got it yet.'

'Isn't that car moving?'

She grabbed my shoulder so that her nails dug in.

22

I screwed my eyes up, watching the black shadow underneath the dirty vehicle and measuring it from a stone that stuck up through the sunbaked mud of the road.

'No,' I said. 'It's Ferdi, walking alongside it. It's him going back, not the car coming forward.'

'It's going to. I'm sure.'

'You'd better let go this arm. I use my gun with that.'

It was quite a good gun. I had fired it twice already. Someone had looked after it since it had been stolen from some government department, possibly the army.

And then the government mark struck me a blow. Up to then with things 'all in a rush' as they certainly had been, I hadn't paid attention to irrelevant details.

'This is a British possession,' I said. 'Bloody W.D. arrow on it. Where did it come from? Must have been smuggled in.'

'Gibraltar, probably,' she said, staring. 'It is moving. Look!'

It was. As I saw it creep forward it

reached the upthrown stone and came over it. From that creep it began to gather speed very slowly, and in the hot silence of the afternoon we could hear the rumble of the tyres.

'It's just rolling,' I said. 'And the doors are still open. This must be it.'

It was it all right. As the car gathered a little speed shots suddenly broke out from across the road. I shoved her back against the wall beside the window and got into its shelter myself.

The men over the road were firing to cover the approach of the car.

I spotted the flame from a gun firing in the window of the house at the left, took aim at it and fired. There was an interval as bullets spattered the plaster outside and then shattered a couple of slats.

It was then that a man fell clean through the rotten shutters across the road and dropped into the dusty road.

The car, doors open came swerving by and ran over his neck with a sick bump as it curved across the road from that house to ours.

I saw the bedroom stripper suddenly

dive head-first out into the dust, leaving the car rolling in between him and me. His steering job was done.

The car crashed into our wall, stuck skew-wise across the opening by which we had driven in. The only opening by which we could drive out.

Having grunched to a halt against the wall it suddenly burst, throwing fire high into the air and up the walls of our house.

The burn was on at last.

2

'It'll burn the house down!' she said, gripping my arm tightly.

I could feel her trembling slightly as she held on and I tried to see down the acute angle the window made with the burning car to the left of it.

It seemed to be jammed into the yard entrance where I had driven my car in. Flames were shooting out of it in all directions from its wide open doors. It looked as if a fire bomb had been let off inside it.

Great splats of burning gas plastered the front of the house and started to catch where wood laths were exposed by the rotten, broken plaster.

The firing from across the street had stopped. The bedroom stripper who had guided the car to the entrance was running down the street behind the blaze, too far off to be shot at.

'It's a try to burn us out,' I said,

watching the wall beside the window.

What stuff the bursting bomb was made of I don't know, but it seemed that the big splats of flame smacked against the walls and stayed there burning. It had caught in many places.

One burst of fire hit the wooden shutters of the window we stood beside and that was that. In an instant every slat of the rotten thing was ablaze.

'What are we going to do?' she said.

'We'll have to do as they want,' I said. 'Get out of the damn place before it burns down on us! Come on and do as you're told. No messing!'

'All right!' She backed suddenly as a great gust of flame blazed into the room as if somebody had opened a furnace door.

Smoke was rushing through the house now, a mixture of acrid wood and paint smoke mixed with the foul chemical smell of the burning fire stuff.

I grabbed her hand and dragged her past the blazing opening to the door. In the hall beyond fire was roaring through cracks in the old front door, and within a minute it would be right inside, burning up the whole of the dry, rotten structure.

We ran out under the overhanging upper floor over the yard. My Mercedes was there still, lurking round the corner of the wall. As I ran towards it she held back.

'You can't get it out!' she gasped.

'We've got to try,' I said. 'Get in the blasted thing and don't argue.'

I had a door open and still she hung back. I pushed her in the bottom and she went in head-first. I bundled her legs in after her, got in beside her and slammed the door.

'You're off your nut!' she panted, twisting round and sitting up. 'That car's jammed in the way out and burning like a bomb!'

'Well, there's no other way, so sit tight and say some prayers. You'll need 'em.'

I started up and sent the car crawling along the side of the rounded house wall until I could see the burning car at the end.

The fire was still blazing out of the open doors and did not seem to have got into the engine. But it wouldn't be many minutes before it did.

The wheels were still steering into our exit.

'What follows is bound to be exciting,' I said, 'but I don't guarantee it'll work, so be ready to dive out and make a run if it doesn't. I'll cover you with the gun.'

I drove at the flaming Peugeot, slowing down as we got up to it. The bumpers grunched and the burning wagon shook, so that the flames wavered in the hot, smoking air.

The Merc took off smoothly. The Peugeot shuddered as it crunched the wall it was jammed against and then freed and ran back ahead of us.

The fire started to pour over the bonnet towards us. I accelerated, shoving the other car fast and hoping the castor action would work my way.

It did. When I straightened the other car swerved either way as we pushed it, but straightened enough to go on up the street.

The fire was blazing over our roof as we shoved it faster. I saw a couple of shot holes appear in the Peugeot windscreen, which suddenly went white, opaque and disappeared in a shower of dust. Fire poured out of the hole, driving straight at us.

'Gosh! Gosh! Gosh!' I heard her panting out the solitary word as she beat the seat with her fist.

I couldn't see past the blazing wreck. I steered by the ragged line of the house roofs on the right.

Then suddenly the flames wavered over to our left as some unexpected draught took it, and I could see a way down the right-hand side of the street. I saw the bedroom stripper crouching in a doorway.

I saw Ferdi standing over him, taking aim with a rifle, waiting for the moment when I would come within an easy shot.

He raised the rifle.

I turned the wheel hard over left. The Merc slid to the left of the Peugeot and shoved it with a sudden last lurch. The burning car swung round backwards towards Ferdi.

As we went by the flaming wreck struck the wall of a house and seemed to burst.

How much stuff there was in it I don't know, but now the petrol tank had gone into the grand display. The flames showered everything. Splats of flame spotted our bonnet as we fled, leaving the smoke and flame behind.

There were also two running men in the street.

The girl cheered. Too soon.

A couple of shots went through our side window and out through the windscreen before we slewed round the end house. Another car was parked there with a man sitting in it.

The big fault I made then was to go by and leave him sitting there with his mouth open. I should have put a shot through him as we went by.

But escape seemed the first requirement. Fire had driven us into trying a breakout and, thanks to the burning vehicle, it had worked. If that hadn't covered us with its umbrella of smoke and fire, we should have been shot like sitting ducks.

Ahead of us then the dusty road wound through scrub and rocks down the falling side of the purple mountain which had destroyed the village.

'They're coming!' she said. 'Step on it!'

'You must be joking!' I said.

Already we were sliding and rolling in the dust which was as deep as sand on a dry beach. It needed care to avoid sliding right out and into one of the rocks. That would cause a hiatus in our flight the pursuers would make use of.

'How many men in the car?' I said.

'Can't see — it's skidding about all over the shop,' she said. 'I think it's two. I think — '

She shut up as we lost grip and went round almost broadside before I pulled out and went on again, leaving enough dust behind to blot out every sign of the following car.

We had already come up this road, but coming up was easier than going down, as the steepness increased.

Apart from the shiffing of the tyres in the dust there came another sound, like somebody whipping the air with a flag.

I couldn't make out what it was until at one savage slide when we came almost to a stop, I saw smoke coming out from under the front wing.

'Bloody tyre's on fire!' I said.

'What are you going to do?' she cried. 'There's no turning off this road, is there?'

'I don't remember one,' I said.

The road steepened more and was hairpinning a couple of times below us. I felt like a snake looking back at its own coils.

The burning tyre was going to stop us very soon. It would probably burst and fly to bits. At that point the men behind could come up at their leisure. I didn't mention it to the girl.

I glanced down the scrub and rock covered slope to the hairpin below us. There was a stream running along by the road down there, a flattish run in between waterfalls.

'Adjust your seat belt!' I shouted at her.

She fumbled for the ends and snapped them across her as the moment arrived to make the decision. The smoke was black and thick as it poured from the front wheel.

Another mile would be its lot, and it was a couple of miles down to the stream along the road.

The risk had to be taken, and there was a hope the followers wouldn't take it.

I swung off the dusty road and started the hair-raising descent down between the bushes and rocks, rocking, rolling, sliding, spinning the wheel to avoid disaster like a dodgem car at a fair.

There was no time to see what had happened to them. From our attitudes and the wildness of the ride it could have looked as if we had slid right off the road and just gone down out of control.

Bushes tore and flew into the air around us as we slithered on down. If it got any steeper we should indeed be out of control. Already the car seemed to be standing on its nose in the crazy run down.

Now and again the girl squeaked but she held on.

The nearer we got to the water the steeper the mad drop went. Twice we grunched rocks along the side and there was no longer any point in trying to steer between bushes. We just missed rocks and tore bushes up whole.

There was no skill about it. It was brute force, ignorance and sheer luck. Twice we broadsided and almost rolled over down the slope, but miracles were on our side.

We got to the flat little stream and turned madly along it in a burst of spray that drenched the screen. I drove along in the water quite slowly and bursts of steam came up from the burning tyre.

I turned my head to look up the towering slope and for a moment I couldn't believe we had actually come down such a precipice.

At the top the roof of the car showed and I saw two men standing there, looking down on us.

It seemed for the moment they could not see us, but then they did. Obviously, until then they thought we must have crashed, but now they saw us driving along the stream one man pointed.

The other pushed him back, they turned and became just a pair of heads. They vanished and the car roof rocked.

They were coming on after us.

'What's your name — Jehu?' the girl said, breathlessly. 'Great conks! That must be the ride of all nightmares!'

I stopped and got out beside the stream. The tyre was black, but it wasn't burning. I got back in.

'It'll have to last a bit,' I said. 'No time to change.'

She didn't see any joke. Nor did I. That tyre wouldn't go far before it went off with a loud bang, but we just had to keep going till then.

We got back on to the road and let go once more. We had gained a lot on the pursuers, almost a couple of miles, even after the stop.

The scrub grew high on either side but here and there she could see down the slope to where the road curled on below.

We were making good speed when she called out.

'There's something coming up!'

'What kind of something?'

'Looks like a big truck. Yes, it is. Very big.'

'We can't pass it,' I said. 'The road's too narrow.'

'Better try a little more rock dodging,' she said.

'They're too thick down here. What would a truck be coming up to a deserted village for?'

'It must be to do with them!'

'That's what it would seem. Take another look when the bushes break.'

We sped on, sliding and grinding along in the dust. She got a good look a quarter mile further on.

'Yes, it's a big truck and going like mad!'

'In a hurry, is it? Then it must be theirs. Which means we're a meat sandwich.'

'I remember a sort of quarry somewhere along here,' she said. 'We might hide.'

'We might if the truck hasn't passed it,' I said grimly. 'But remember they can see our dust from above. Must look like a steam locomotive from behind.'

'It was one of these bends,' she said.

'They all look the damn same to me. How's the truck doing?'

'It's coming still,' she said.

Those simple words had a chill on

them. The road was narrow and bounded by rocks instead of just scrub so that when we met the truck that would be it.

'How far off is it?'

'Two bends down.'

'Is that all? Hell!'

★ ★ ★

A bend ahead of us ran by a gap in rock cliffs with a lot of bush on the bend itself.

'There!' she said. 'That's it!'

It wasn't surprising I hadn't noticed it in the helter-skelter charge we had made up here. We could see the cutting of a quarry between the gap in the cliffs.

The entrance was so overgrown it looked as if there was no gap there. She looked back but the pursuing car was not in sight. The truck was still grinding up the pass below us, but how near was a matter of guesswork.

I slowed down and charged the bush, praying fallen rock had not got sprayed on to the old track into the quarry. We hit a lot of bush into the air and

38

bumped and rolled.

Suddenly we weren't on the ground any more. It was an appalling sensation, a sudden silence and our stomachs dropped away right out of our boots.

Then a thump, soft, pillowy, pulling us to a standstill in a cloud of flying sand. I looked back. We had fallen about four feet into a small mountain of sand. A ledge of ground, rising sharply, rose up to the bushes we had broken through. There were a lot of bush bits lying around in the sand, but the main bushes had closed behind us.

I stopped the engine and got out.

In the soft heat we heard the harsh whine of the truck gears getting louder. Then there was another sound, the humming of a car engine rising up as the wheels spun on the dust road.

Then brakes squealing; whose we only guessed at. But there was no crash, just the harsh squeaking of the discs on the car and the grunting hissing of the air brakes on the truck. Then almost a silence, with the truck diesel motor rattling, and a shrill swearing in Spanish.

'Did you let a car go by?' we heard Ferdi say.

'No. What car?'

'Well, it can't have disappeared!'

'I kept telling you,' a third man said, 'they never came back on the road after taking the drop down. That's what. Back up there again. That's where they are.'

'Switch your motor off and wait here,' Ferdi said.

The truck engine stopped and then we heard the car screaming backwards up the road again. The camouflage of the gap must have been very good. Obviously nearly all had sprung back after it had let us through.

But if someone took a close look, they must surely find enough signs to lead him down to where we lay in the quarry.

It wasn't big, about a hundred yards across and with its walls rising to about three hundred feet in rocky steps above us. There were entrances to tunnels and the old broken track of tramways running into them.

It provided a warren to hide in, but we couldn't hide the car. The bet was on how long it would be before they examined the broken bushes up there.

We heard a man whistling, and then another man spoke.

'How long will he be?'

'How do I know?'

'I want to get on up there with load in this heat. I don't like it.'

'You get paid danger money.'

The conversations all took place in English. The two up by the truck sounded Cockney or Australian, but neither was marked enough to be sure.

'All the same, I never like this kind of load.'

'What the hell? If it blew you wouldn't know anything.'

The girl was crouching by me listening intently, as if trying to recognise who they were.

'That sense of humour belongs in the morgue,' the second man said. 'That's always the trouble with a bloody pommie. Queer sense of humour.'

'You've got to die sometime, Digger. Some ways are better than others. The Big Bang theory suits me.'

'It suits me, too, Pommie, but not now, I tell yer. Not bloody now!' There was a pause, then he went on, 'If that little lot starts sweatin', cobber, you'll — '

'Ah, shut up. You make me nervous, gabbin' on like that. I been handlin' that stuff for twenty years. Back in England I got my explosives licence still.'

'If you turned up there, cobber, you'd have another kind of licence tacked on yer suit. I want to get movin'. What are they up to?'

'Lookin'. They had that tart up there.'

'Christ! Don't say they let her go!'

She hugged close to me, grabbing my arm tightly.

'She didn't have a car, did she?'

'She could pick one up. Look, she was dead set on gettin' here. Ferdi said.'

I glanced at her. She pretended not to find anything of importance in the remark.

'She couldn't do anything by herself, Digger. She'd have to have a man with her.'

'Well, if she picked up a car maybe she picked up a man inside it, too. What's so impossible?'

Somebody spat.

'You unnerve me,' said the pommie.

There was a pause.

'Where the hell are they?' Digger said. 'I don't like it here in this heat!'

'Sit on it! They'll be back!'

'Okay, okay. But if we're moving you get the air through. That keeps things fresh. Remember, they said about this stuff not being like the old, low grade jelly.'

'I've handled it all,' the pommie said. 'It ain't that hot.'

There was the sound of a cab door opening, then slammed.

'The thermometer in there says hot enough,' Digger said. 'Why in hell don't they come back?'

A match scratched.

'Do you have to smoke and all?' Digger shouted.

'I'm downwind, yer silly bastard,' the pommie said.

'I can hear 'em up there somewhere,' Digger said, after a while. 'Beatin' the bush. What the hell? I thought he said it was a car they'd lost?'

'He knows what he's doing.'

'What that bloody Pork-and-Beans-G.I. job?' scoffed Digger. 'If it's talk you want, he's the big sell. As for knowin' anything, that's another shelf, matey.'

'He just happens to be boss.'

'Well, all right, so he is. That don't make him clever.'

'It makes him boss,' said the pommie.

It was drenching hot where we were. The moment of discovery of my car could not be far ahead, and the sensible move was to get into one of the tunnels.

But I didn't want to give up the chance of overhearing what might be said next, and when Ferdi came back, though the latter would be almost dead on the moment when they would find the car.

I started to back across the sand, pulling her with me. It was very still but the walls of rock around us shimmered as if made of printed on shiver-thin Polythene. 'Where to?' she breathed.

'Nearer the bolt holes,' I whispered back.

We got down behind a mass of scrub growing up in the middle of one set of tram rails.

'For gawd's sake, they must give in soon,' Digger grumbled. His voice came clear in the silent heat.

'Shuddup.' The pommie sounded hot and disagreeable now. He might have been beginning to catch Digger's anxiety over the load. 'They'll be back.'

Somebody began to eat something. It sounded like an apple. It helped a lot. We backed on to the wall of rock near a tunnel mouth until the apple chomping could just be heard. There we stayed.

From somewhere up the hill a motor horn sounded, beeped three times.

'What's he callin' for?' Digger said.

'Us, I reckon,' the pommie said. 'Get up.'

The cab doors slammed and the big oil engine groaned and started up. The truck began to whine on again through the dust, rubbing its heavy double wheels over the vague tracks we must have made. It drew away up the hill. 'Now what?' she said.

'Now you answer me questions,' I said. 'Those jimps knew you were coming up here. How did they know that?'

'They're guessing,' she said.

'They *knew*,' I said. 'What's more you led me up into this death trap deliberately, and all along I've thought it was just the result of trying to escape.'

'You wouldn't believe a couple of thugs like that before me, would you?' she said, almost plaintively.

'Yes,' I said.

'What do you think they've found up there?' she said.

'What did you expect to find up here? The land on that map?'

'This map,' she said, touching her shirt front, 'is just a splendid piece of élite cartography. Nothing more.'

'Oh, for heaven's sake! Let me look at it now there's time.'

She pulled it out and would have handed it over but jerked it back again.

'Listen!' she said, big-eyed. 'They've stopped.'

We listened. The diesel was throbbing very faintly in the distance up the road.

'They've met the car, that's all,' I said.

'Yes, but there's a car coming down from over here!'

She pointed up over the opposite edge of the rock face a hundred yards across the gap. We listened together. A car was coming down the mountain road from the village.

'The villains are foreclosing,' I said. 'They must have had a couple of personnel wagons up there, not just the one.'

I saw a heap of stuff nearby. It was a lot of sacks and old wooden poles.

'Let's cover the car,' I said. 'It might give us a lot more time.'

We got a lot of sacks, leant poles against and across the car then covered it all with sacks. An old shovel put a lot of sand over that, so it didn't look a recent heap.

When it was done I was almost melting with the heat. We went back behind the tram scrub. There was a confused sound of car engines from up the hill, but they painted no mental picture of what might be happening up there.

'They're searching all the way down to here,' she said. 'That's what.'

'Show me the map.'

She tried desperately to think of something to change the subject. I could see that by the way her eyes looked all round as if trying to find a subject floating nearby.

'Come on,' I said.

So she gave it to me. I unrolled and looked at it closely. It was some damn map for a hundred pounds. It had been drawn by a German with a pencil and he had been no hand at art, cartography or anything but rough sketching.

Efforts had been made to clarify certain details by writing a descriptive word in a hand that was scarcely legible.

It remained a vague impression of road, hill, stream, valley, some x's parked about.

'What in hell is it?' I said. 'Where's the value?'

'It's an original by Gauguin,' she said.

'He wasn't German.'

'He refused to speak French after they threw him out.'

'Listen, what is so important about this that these men will run big risks to get it? And why do you take such risks to keep it?'

'Didn't I tell you? Buried treasure,' she said, and grinned. 'The parchment is interesting. It's human skin.'

'If you don't tell me the truth,' I said, 'I'll throw you out on the road in front of these men when they get back down here.'

'You wouldn't!' she said, startled.

'Why the hell wouldn't I? I'm tired of taking risks with my neck for the sake of a half-wit girl. I don't see the point, or the value.'

'I keep telling you. It's buried treasure!' She looked really hard done by then, lip biting and all.

'Don't cry, for heaven's sake!' I said. 'The act's good enough as it is.'

'They're coming back,' she said suddenly and pointed up to the gap.

The thump and grind of the truck was getting louder in the heat, but running against the cogs, running backwards down the hill.

The whining eased and then stopped. We heard the cab doors grunch open and then slam.

'Could be through the bushes,' the

pommie said. 'Shove through and see.'

'I can't stand it!' she hissed and then to my horror I saw her put her head back and start to let out a scream.

3

The first dulcet, tearing note of that scream hit the sky as I clamped my fist over her face. She struggled, but the situation was too brisk to let her free and I locked her up in my grip and picked her off the ground, kicking.

She kicked all the way into the mouth of the old tunnel, and then I shoved her up against the wall, keeping my hand over her mouth, and suddenly she slacked off.

From beyond the bushes I heard the pommie shout.

'What's that?'

'Some kind of bird,' Digger replied. 'You get eagles up in these mountains.'

'Sounded funny to me. Behind them bushes.'

We waited. Her eyes were big, staring at me over my hand.

The sound of bushes being brushed aside came dry and crackly, and then, peering round the edge of the tunnel

51

mouth, I saw a man's head above the bushes.

He stared round the place and down to the mound under which we had hidden the car. But he turned his head past it in his broad scan of the quarry.

'Don't see anything,' he called back. 'But it sounded like a dame yelling.'

'If it's that tart, it must have come from up the hill. She's somewheres up there, Ferdi's sure they ditched the car down a crevasse and ducked. They had a tyre on fire.'

The pommie shrugged, turned and I saw no more of him in that scene. I hoped to hear the truck start and go away out of it, but the men's voices continued, too far off for me to tell what was being said.

'Going to be quiet?' I said.

She nodded as best she could, and I took my hand away.

'You nearly smothered me,' she said, touching her lips.

'Pity I didn't. What in hell did you do that for?'

'To start things moving. I get so that I just can't stand around any longer. I have to get going or scream.'

'Don't scream any more, or I'll wring your neck.'

She didn't say anything but shook her head, looking big-eyed and childish.

'Will they go?' she whispered.

'What's the good of guessing? The thing that interests me most is that they knew you would come up here, and they were organised to come up here, and they want that map. So what's on the map is up here somewhere.'

A faint cunning light came into her dark eyes.

'Perhaps it is,' she said.

'The map is so bad it could be anywhere almost.'

'Perhaps they didn't want it to be too obvious,' she said. 'After all, it is buried treasure.'

'Well, they've got a truckful of jelly or somewhat the same. The pommie sounded like a miner because miners have explosive certificates at home. So things begin to tie up.'

There was some more shouting from the road, both near and distant as if the car searchers were coming down away from searching the scrub.

'The funny point is,' I said, 'when Ferdi told us to come out of that house he didn't mention the map. If I'd been in his position, I'd have said throw out the map. When it was thrown out I'd set fire to the house and burn you up.'

'You're just a plain villain,' she said.

'Well, wouldn't you do that?'

'Perhaps.'

'Why didn't Ferdi? 'Is it possible he didn't know you had it till you came rushing up here?'

'How do I know what Ferdi knows?'

She was the most unhelpful rescued heroine I ever came across. I constantly had the feeling she was trying to put one over on me as well as on anyone else who came into the scene.

The tunnel we were in was shored with props and curved round out of sight forty yards behind us, the twin uneven rails of the tramway following the curve out of sight.

'Do you know this part of the world?' I said.

'I come to Santander now and again.'

'I mean this particular area.'

'No. I don't remember ever coming here.'

'But you know about the place.'

'I heard about it.'

'From your girl-friend with the maps and guns?'

'She's interested in the old mining areas. She took Geography also Geology. She's a true rock head.'

We listened to the sounds of distant shouting, but it gave no clue as to what was going on up there.

'Soon they'll have to take a closer look down here,' I said.

'Why? We could be miles away by now.'

'But the car can't. That's what they're looking for. They think we'll be somewhere near it. They'll be damn right.'

'We can run further in,' she said.

'So long as there isn't a blocked end. Old mines have a habit of falling in once the timbers rot.'

'You go and look, then.'

'Sure,' I said and grabbed her hand. 'You come too in case you scream again.'

She looked sulky, but after a moment dragging back, she came. The tunnel was big enough for the daylight to get round the bend and into a wide gallery which seemed like a tramway junction. There were five tunnels radiating from it, and further than that we could not see.

'It'll do,' I said.

We went back to the mouth. The sounds from the searchers had stopped.

'They haven't gone, have they?' she whispered.

'I shouldn't think so.'

We listened, heard nothing but some birds high up near the peaks. The world seemed empty but for us.

'They must have gone,' she said, cocking her head.

'If they had we should hear gears in the distance. There's nothing.'

'Then what's happening?'

'We're listening for them. Perhaps they're doing the same about us.'

'I don't like it.'

'Nobody's desperately keen.'

There came the sudden whump of the diesel starter and then the rattle of the engine. But when the whine of gears began it sounded like the noise they had made when the truck had backed down from further up the hill.

'It's going downwards,' I said. 'What's the idea now?'

'To get somewhere the car can get by,' she said.

'Why should the car go down? They know we're somewhere above the truck, not below it.'

The whining grew a little fainter. The vehicle was going very slowly down. I didn't hear anything of Ferdi's car following it, or even coming down from up the hill.

The whining of the truck in reverse grew very faint and then stopped, almost as if it had driven into a tunnel which had absorbed its noise.

No sound of the car coming down.

'They've all gone,' she said impulsively and went to go out of the tunnel we were in.

I grabbed her forearm and pulled her back.

'Think before you leap,' I said.

'But they've gone!'

'They could be up there, the other side of the bushes,' I said. 'The car could have come down when we were back in the earthworks.'

She made an effort to tear away and run, but by then I was getting used to her little ways and I had my other hand ready to catch her hard, swing her back and let her go again, behind me in the tunnel.

'A reason for lying low could be to make us think they've gone and go out to see,' I said.

'But we can't just stay here!' she protested.

'We'll have to wait,' I said.

'But you don't understand — '

She started off on that line, but choked it off and stared at me with those big eyes, as if she had frightened herself.

'Understand what?' Suspicion was on me again.

She thought quickly, obviously searching again.

'I mean — if we stay here they're bound to come back, aren't they?' She was breathless.

'What don't I understand?' I persisted.
'Just what I said!'

'Tell me what I don't understand or I'll drag you up there and chuck you out in front of them. I mean it! I'm sick of this doublecross — '

'No, no! It isn't!' she said and slung her arms round my neck. 'Don't keep saying things about me! It isn't fair!'

I got her arms and undid them from my neck. She looked surprised that her love hold hadn't worked. She was a very spoilt girl.

She came to the point of blowing up in my face. I saw the blazing danger light in her eyes, and then something over her shoulder caught my eye.

The bushes up above the car had moved.

I shoved her back against the tunnel wall.

'Quiet! Visitors!' I whispered.

She went stiff, then began to move along the wall towards the tram centre. I let her go, but she stopped a few yards from me.

'Who is it?' she whispered.

59

'Ferdi.'

Ferdi stood at the top of the four foot drop, an automatic rifle in his hands. It seemed to be his constant companion, for I had never seen him without it. He looked around the quarry, his head turning slowly in intense search.

Having scanned all round twice, his eyes turned back to the tunnel mouths. He stayed, looking in our direction, then raised the gun above his head and dropped down into the sand.

He did not look at the heap of car, but stared straight ahead. She began to whisper something. I raised a finger and she stopped.

The pistol was in my hand then, but round the edge of the tunnel shoring I could see Ferdi, and he couldn't see me as he came on, creeping stealthily, the gun ready in his hands now.

I shoved the gun into my pocket and went right to the edge of the mouth.

He came on. I got back so that I was in the reveal formed by the post standing clear of the wall.

He stopped outside the mouth, then

looked away to the other tunnels. In that moment I threw my handkerchief down in the middle of the entrance.

He looked back and saw it, white as snow in the hot sun.

I saw his hands tighten on the gun, and then he came in, creeping, watchful, but not watchful enough.

It was easy. I got him from the side with a lock of one arm under his chin and a grip on his right wrist that would break it if he tried to force against it.

'Drop the gun,' I said.

He stayed still and stiff in my hold. I tightened the lock almost till his apple cracked.

'Drop the gun or I'll break your neck!'

Another moment of stiffness, then I felt him relax. The gun fell in between the tram tracks. The girl ran forward and picked it up.

In that movement as I recorded it, she struck me as being used to such weapons.

I threw Ferdi against the wall so his back smashed into it and knocked the breath out of him. He sagged against the rock.

'Where are the others? And don't raise

your voice,' I said.

He went to pick up his hat which had come off and lay on the rails.

'Leave that. You won't need it. Where are the others?'

He straightened again, watching me with eyes so dark they were almost black, like currants.

'One on the road. The truckmen have gone back.'

'Back where?'

He shrugged.

'Where?' I said, and hit him.

It was a double knock, for I knocked his head back and the wall hit his head. He seemed dazed, and shook his noggin as if that might shake away pain.

'Where?'

'The village down there on the road,' he said.

'Have they gone to fetch anyone?'

He waited a bit, and then saw me raise my fist again.

'No.'

'What have they gone for?'

'To block this road way down below. It goes through the pass down there. You wouldn't get through without being seen.'

'Seems simple enough,' I said.

He looked dazed and shook his head again.

'Let's talk some more, shall we?'

He just stared as if he didn't quite understand.

'Why do you want this girl?' I said.

His eyes swivelled to her. She seemed to be trying to stare him out. There was an odd moment of silence.

'She has something which is mine,' he said, looking back at me.

'You mean that she stole it?'

'Yes.'

'What proof have you got?'

'She picked my pocket.'

'You liar!' she shouted.

This was a difficult situation, for my uneasiness over her erratic behaviour, and knowing what a spoilt child she was, made me think that this could possibly be the truth.

She went to hit him with the gun in a fit of extreme temper. I got her just in time, and held her arms to her sides until she got tired of wriggling. Then I let go.

*   *   *

'Don't let's fight,' I said, and turned back to Ferdi. 'Tell me about this crime.'

'We danced,' he said sullenly. 'It was a frame up. She picked my pocket.'

'Of what?'

He shrugged.

'You're not suggesting she stole money?'

'What else is there?' he said.

'And because of this you chase her up into the mountains, firing shots all the way, then try to burn us alive?' I said. 'Quite some money, by the sound of it.'

He said nothing. She started off again.

'It's all lies. Surely you can tell that? How could I know what he had in his horrid pockets? I never saw him before we danced. And he asked me. So what?'

Ferdi started to laugh, but it was a short effort, and looked as if it made his head ache.

All the time I kept an eye flicking to the corner of the mouth and the bushes up there above the car. The other man must come soon to find what had happened to Ferdi.

'Let's not beat around,' I said. 'It was a map she stole.'

He just looked at me.

'I want to know what that map means,' I went on.

Again he shrugged.

'It could mean nothing,' he said. 'It is old and gone through many hands.'

This unexpected openness took me by surprise.

'How old?'

'The skin is yellow,' he said. 'It was part of a lamp shade.'

The girl was watching me now as if to see my reaction that at least one thing she'd said was corroborated.

'You're lining up with a German concentration camp of a long time ago,' I said.

'Could be,' he said, watching me. 'Let me talk to you now.'

'Do that.'

'You must be an adventurer,' he said. 'Nobody but an experienced escaper could have shoved that car out of the way like that. Nobody but an experienced man would have thought of it. And

coming down over the side of the hill — '
His eyes were very sharp now. 'We are all
men of that kind. We take risks. We live in
danger, but we reap good rewards.'

She came close to my side, glancing
from me to Ferdi, trying to watch for
collusion. If it showed, she would jump
on it. I could tell that instinctively.

'What's the proposition?' I said, to
bring her on.

'Come in,' he said. 'Join us. There will
be enough to share.'

'Don't listen to him,' she said urgently.
'It's a trick. He's just pretending to be
friendly. Don't believe him!'

'What's the guarantee?' I said, shoving
her away.

'Don't listen!' she cried.

'Shut up!' I said. 'I've stood about all I
want from you. You've put me in this
mess, nearly got me killed over and over,
so now it's my turn to sign an armistice.
Keep quiet.'

She looked taken aback. She must have
been for she drew a sharp breath of rage,
but didn't say anything.

'I can't guarantee,' Ferdi said. 'You

have to trust, that's all.'

'But what about the others? Will they want to share?'

'They do as I say,' Ferdi said.

'You're a fool to listen!' she burst out again. 'He's just a cheap crook. You can't trust a man like him! Why do you think he's turning round like this? Only to make you think everything's all right, then he'll shoot you in the back. I know him!'

'But you said you didn't,' I reminded her. 'You said you danced and talked. That isn't enough to let anybody get to know a man.'

Ferdi laughed. It was a short, brutal little sound.

'I can weigh them up as well as you,' she said.

For some reason she dropped it there.

'Think about it,' Ferdi said. 'You can't get away from here without me. You have a saying, 'If you can't beat 'em, join 'em'. This seems like a time to do just that.'

He put the facts quite succinctly. There could be a dozen ways out of this place, but they might need mountain climber's equipment, and certainly a local map, which we hadn't got.

Otherwise there was only the road which wound down the pass, and I seemed to remember a bottleneck in the pass when we had come up.

I didn't think Ferdi would lie about that bottleneck being an easy place for two men and a truck to hold. He didn't strike me as being a man to play cards he didn't have.

It was a way out, but it would mean a doublecrosser's way. It would mean going in with a double-dyed gang of four killers, playing along with them and then ditching them.

It was the ditching that might not be possible, for once I was in, they would watch me because they certainly wouldn't trust me.

What chance would there be then of a double quick twist that would defeat all four with guns at the ready?

Perhaps alone my chances might be long odds, but with the girl they were astronomical.

Another point was that the crooks

obviously had business up the hill, perhaps back almost into the deserted village. That was where the girl had led them, and me.

To be taken up there again, that overhung dead end, with the crooks in command of the only way down seemed like having my head in a noose they could tighten at will.

On the other hand, I might use Ferdi as a hostage.

Then I recalled the truckmen's talk about Ferdi and I wasn't so sure they would value Ferdi as highly as to mean some sacrifice to themselves.

Or I could down Ferdi here and now, then go out and try to down the man on the road. That might succeed.

But it still left the escape route commanded by the enemy at the bottom end.

At this point of decision, the girl stirred it up all over again.

She turned, gave a short laugh, and then ran full pelt away down the tunnel, still holding the rifle.

Both Ferdi and I glanced as she fled,

then we looked at each other. Again he shrugged. He said more by shrugging than any other means, it seemed.

But then he did speak, surprisingly.

'Better follow,' he said. 'You don't know her.'

The sound of her boots was echoing faintly in the tunnels so that you couldn't tell sound from echo.

I had come to bring her back, lunatic as she now seemed to be, and this of all times, was not the one to change my mind in.

'After you,' I said.

He laughed then and as he turned his back on me his eyes were the last to go. As if he knew I was being taken for a looney's ride through all this.

We went on along the tram-tracks. He kept his hands at his sides. I had taken the precaution of showing him my gun just before that final laughing turn away.

We came to the junction. Apart from a couple of old tipper trucks standing on one lot of lines, the place was empty.

He stopped.

'You say,' he said.

We stood in silence, listening. The faint

little thump of the boots still echoed, but it was impossible to tell from which tunnel it came.

The light wasn't really good enough to tell which marks in the old dust were new and which had been there years.

'I think that one,' Ferdi said.

Of course. He was keen to follow. She still had the map.

The marks there looked a little more disturbed than the others.

'May I offer you a light?' he said, and laughed again.

'Tell me where. I'll get it,' I said.

'Side pocket of my coat,' he said.

I reached in and found a small flashlight. It shone well down the chosen tunnel. We followed the light. The tunnel turned several times as we tramped the dusty floor between the tracks.

Often we stopped to listen. Now and again we heard the little sound of the boots, which seemed to prove this was the tunnel she had gone down, but after a while there was silence.

We stayed there, and there was no more sound of her.

'Well?' he said. It was mocking.

'She's nutty,' I said. 'She'll never find the way out again. Why? Why run?'

I was completely bewildered by this act on her part, though, as I was to see, it all knitted into the pattern of the rest.

'She wishes to be alone,' he said.

'Are you another nut?'

Once more the shrug.

'You do not know this girl. She means to be alone. If you had not come to the hotel, you would not have seen her at all.'

'You seem to know the lot,' I said.

He sighed.

'If only one could,' he said. 'But with these amateurs it is almost impossible. They follow no rules. Every twist, every trick is new.'

'When you happen to have a twisted mind,' I said.

Then he laughed.

'But she has that!' he said. 'She has a limitless capacity for surprises. One does not know where to look to see her next.'

'She could be lost now.'

'She could be. I don't think she is.'

'But she doesn't know the place, does she?'

Again the shrug.

'Are there plans of these old workings?' I said.

'Somewhere, perhaps. I do not know. The mountains have been abandoned a long time now.'

'How in hell shall we find her?'

'I think that she will find us, when she wishes.'

'How well do you know this girl?'

'Since yesterday.'

'And she's been doing this sort of thing all the time?'

'Every bit.'

'She bought that map.'

Shrug.

'It couldn't be a sketch of these workings, could it?' I said.

'It is somewhere here for sure,' he said.

'But she just ran. Simply turned and ran.'

'Is it possible that she recognised something?'

'What was there?'

'I do not know. I am thinking of the

possibility, not the fact.'

I looked either way of the tunnel. It was dark and silent beyond the torch. She had been swallowed up in it completely, sight and sound.

She had deliberately run, without light or guide of any kind, into a labyrinth in the lost mountains, of which it was most likely no plans existed at all. From all I had seen these workings must have been abandoned over thirty years ago.

And yet —

Her headlong flight from the hotel had driven me up here, a place to which she had meant all along to go.

Our downlong flight from the deserted village had ended in this quarry which *she* had remembered at the last minute, after pretending she didn't remember any-where on the way down where we could hide.

Now, after being in the workings a half-hour, she had suddenly run headlong again.

Was this desperate impulse another premeditated travel from A to B? But into the dark! Into the twisting forgotten entrails of a mine that could have swallowed a hundred people and never given them up again!

Was she mad? Or was this sanity painted to look like madness?

This time I found myself shrugging.

4

'Either she's crazy, or she's too clever,' Ferdi said. 'I do not make her out at all.'

'I don't think she had a light,' I said, staring into the dark mouths of the tunnels surrounding us. 'She could have been hysterical and just ran. But I think she's too tough for that.'

'What are you going to do?'

'There is a choice of tunnels. They all look alike and I can see no tracks which she might have left. So what can we do?'

'You cannot leave her?'

He watched me with slitted eyes that shone in the gloom.

I didn't answer that one. I was beginning to wish I could leave her. She was a dead load of trouble for me.

I kept trying to find a reason for her suddenly rushing off headlong into pitch darkness without a light, leaving out madness as the possible reason.

She was not mad. Her behaviour had

been anything but mad. There had been a reason for every unreasonable thing she'd done. I felt there must be some reason for this.

Into the dark of a strange place without a light.

Or was it strange to her?

If I assumed sanity, then I had to assume she did know the place and —

She knew she wouldn't *need* a light.

'I think we'll take them one by one,' I said. 'Just go in a little way and see.'

'Okay. You think so.' He shrugged again.

We went into the first and about forty yards down the uneven ground between the tracks. I switched the light out. It was dark as a grave.

We came back and repeated the performance in the next two.

'Why do you keep turning out the light?' he said quickly.

It hadn't occurred to me that my apparently inexplicable wish for sudden darkness was scaring him.

'Testing,' I said.

In the fourth tunnel we found it. The

light went out as before but this time the darkness did not seem the same. As if there was a pinhole in it somewhere.

'Put the light on!' he said urgently.

I was holding his arm then, and felt it trembling.

'Can you see anything?' I said.

His arm went rigid in my grip and stayed like that for several seconds. Then the muscles relaxed and I heard him breathe out.

'There's light — somewhere,' he said.

'Not behind us. In front somewhere. We're going on.'

'Put the light on, then!'

'No. Feel the way along the wall.'

He hesitated. I shoved him sideways to the wall.

'Go on,' I said and pushed him forwards along it. 'Steer the way.'

He started, wary, clumsy, stopping every other yard as he struck something with his foot. He was worked up, nervous.

The pinhole got no larger or nearer. We stopped after some distance.

'What is it?' he said, breathing hard.

'It's a hole,' I said. 'It must be mustn't

it? What else can it be?'

'It would get nearer. It stays there.'

'It's too small to be sure,' I said.

That was the truth of the matter. It was like a pinhole in a can with a candle burning inside it. You see a pinprick of light, but put the eye nearer and it blurs out, prism-wise. Nearer still and there is just light without shape. The more you strain to judge the shape and distance away the more impossible it gets.

This light point ahead of us was like that, suspended in black nothing.

'Go on further,' I said.

'Suppose there's a hole — ' he started off.

'Feel each step as you go,' I said. 'There's no hurry.'

We went on. He felt each step as if testing for mines.

Still the pinprick seemed remote. It was like trying to walk towards a star. I even began to feel dizzy with the strain of keeping it before my eye like a target.

He kept stopping.

'It's too far,' he said. 'We shall be lost. Put the light on! We cannot tell what galleries we may have passed — '

'None this side, so it doesn't matter,' I said. 'We just turn about and feel our way back. But not yet.'

'What's the good? It cannot be a hole. It must be a trick of the light!'

I was beginning to think that myself, but I realised the fact was that through the stumbling darkness, we had seemed to travel a damn sight farther than we really had. The stop and start, hesitation, fearful footfalls, all helped to make the journey seem long and tense.

Probably the girl had run towards it, knowing that if she kept the pinpoint of light in front of her she wouldn't run into anything.

Then came the big shock. Ferdi stopped.

'Go on!' I said, pushing.

'I cannot! It does not go on!'

I reached out and touched a rough wall dead in front of us. The pinpoint of light which had seemed never to come near was actually within reach of our fingers.

I switched on the light and shut my eyes, opening them slowly. Right in front of us was an old wooden door, wormy and rotten. The light had been coming from a small collection of worms' holes, grouped over a rough circle of a quarter inch across.

Obviously, our long and tedious journey could only have been a few yards, so distorting had been the darkness and the hesitant approach.

The door had only a broken, half-fallen wooden latch as thick as a man's arm. But when pushed and pulled the door didn't move.

'Bolted the other side,' he said, hissing and wiping his sweating face.

'Of course,' I said. 'She went through.'

'What was the light, then?'

'It was so intense it must have been sunlight. There's daylight beyond this door, I'll bet.'

'Break it in!' Ferdi said, recovering from his fear of the dark, perhaps with the idea of daylight beyond the door. 'There is timber about!'

By the light we could see timber about. Some of the roof props had lost their wedges and just lay in the stone dust beside the rusty tracks. They would make good battering rams.

'Get one,' I said.

He went and got one of the props. It was heavy and tough.

'It just needs a little care,' I said. 'In case there's a drop on the other side and the door isn't as tough as it looks.'

He hesitated. Ferdi was very careful of Ferdi, though he had no compunction in setting fire to, shooting at or driving at, anybody else.

'I had not thought. We must take care,' he said.

What made me say that was the tram tracks ended. They did not go on under the door but stopped up against it, and if they didn't go on, there could be a reason in that there was nothing beyond for them to go on on.

'Okay. Let's measure the distance.'

I let him go next the door holding the lead end of the stick. I got behind him and then switched out the light after we had measured the swing from back up to half-way through the forward swing, which would hit the door planks hard.

'Back!' I said, 'and hold it.'

We swung the big timber back, our arms pendulumwise, and then I shouted to swing forward. We swung nicely. The baulk hit the door something hard and the whole rotten structure of planks shook and we saw daylight appear in lines where the planks shook apart. Some of them stayed apart.

We swung again. This time the cracks got wider, but the rotten old structure still held against us.

The third swing was bad. We didn't do it together. We hit the door with the baulk but didn't improve the damage.

The next time I called the stroke, and we got a good shot in. The cracks got wider. The upper part of one plank fell right out and let in a lot of daylight. It was on the hinge side so we couldn't reach the bar that held the door, but it was enough to see through.

'Hold it!' I said.

He stayed there looking at me and laid the timber down.

'Don't run or I'll shoot you in the back,' I said.

He shrugged.

I stretched up and peered through the hole. It was as if one whole side of the original tunnel had fallen clean away, for the left wall stood, and the floor of the tunnel — with tram tracks — ran on, but where the side of the floor ended there was a sheer drop down into a gulley of trees and wild scrub and some old broken, yellowed huts showing their wretched roofs like rafts floating on the undergrowth.

'What is there?'

'Nothing,' I said. 'Some kind of valley. You know the area. Where does it go?'

'You are wrong. I know only the old village. Nothing else. Is it worth it to go on?'

'We have to follow the girl.'

He shrugged.

'Okay.'

He bent and picked up the baulk again. I went in behind him and we swung again. This time we shattered a hole big enough to get my arms through and lift the bar out of its slots.

The door swung out when I pushed it.

'Remember,' he said, hissing again, 'she has the rifle.'

'For God's sake!' I cried. 'She won't shoot me!'

'What of me?' he said, reasonably. 'You will not trust me to go behind. I shall be in front, open.'

'You really think she'd murder you?'

'She is a crazy girl and has a gun,' he said, obstinately. 'Mad girls, mad elephants. What's the difference? Don't stand in their way.'

We stood there looking along the tram ledge. There was a gap in the rail lengths with a small turntable beyond the door. Another set of tracks ran to the right and entered the rock face ten feet away.

It was quiet and deserted. I heard water running somewhere, roaring over a fall. The line ahead ran on the ledge to another tunnel in the sheer rock face.

'She knew of this,' Ferdi said.

'Obviously. But where did she go after she went through the door?'

Looking around it seemed that the valley was mountain locked. It couldn't have been entirely, but it was as far as the eye could see from where we were.

'Don't you have a map?' I said.

He shrugged and went on staring at the secret valley. I knew why he was staring. We could hear the water; somewhere there was a stream.

This could be the valley of the skin map.

★　★　★

'We could shout,' Ferdi said.

'And she'd answer? I don't think she's lost.' I grabbed his arm and forced him forward. 'Out. We must look.'

He hung back, then gave way. He was a great one for trying to get in the back row. I wondered what this latter day Plaza-Torro had in the way of personal magnetism that made him the leader of his small mob.

The pommie had expressed contempt. The digger had sounded as if it was more an idea that he followed than the man.

We started to walk to the straight ahead tunnel. It was quiet with a kind of quiet that seemed to echo. The rushing of the waterfall had dropped back into the background. I heard no birds. Our footfalls on the dusty rock grated. It was impossible to be silent on that stuff.

Ferdi walked slowly.

The thump was not as loud as it should have been. We both swung round. The old door had shut again, battered and torn now, but still a barrier.

'She must be back there!' he said.

'It could just have fallen to,' I said. 'Don't jump around so much. You'll make me nervous soon. We couldn't pass her in the dark unless I had a cold, which I haven't.'

'Why do you be so sure? You can't be — '

'She wears scent. I'm surprised you didn't notice.'

'I did not think.'

'You should. You have men depending on you doing the thinking.'

The germ of an idea of using Ferdi was coming into my mind the more I saw of his wriggling little character. He was a born back-stabber, which was why he always looked behind him and hung back from going ahead.

The idea was born then, but before I could get ahead with it, I had to know something of how Ferdi had come to be in command of his band.

All I could think of was money.

That was the simple solution which fitted all conditions, provided I could know that he had some.

I stopped and leant against the rock wall, looking out over the valley. I offered him a cigarette and I had one too. He looked uneasy about smoking it, as if the smoke might draw attention from some hiding place.

'I've been thinking of your offer,' I said.

'Ah!' He looked suddenly eager.

'Contrary to your supposition,' I said, 'I'm a businessman. I deal in hard bargains. I take risks only when it seems I can scoop the pool. Think of me like that, and then make me an offer.'

'I have told you, you cannot get out of this place without me,' he said quickly. 'My men are in control.'

'That card isn't so good now,' I said. 'There could be a way out on this side.'

'Pah! You can see it is surrounded! Mountains all round. Just a freak depression.'

'But we got here through a tunnel,' I said. 'There are lots of tunnels.'

'True. Enough to be lost in forever,' he said sharply.

'I admit you have a card, but I'm pointing out you can't be sure it isn't trumped.'

'We will assume that it is good. I know more of the country than you.'

'Put the proposition.'

'You come with us for a share. We need another man who knows how to act.'

'Oh!' I said and watched him. 'You mean that you have rivals here?'

'It is possible. Anything is possible.'

'I see. But you're a long time coming to your offer. Is it changing? First of all I thought you would offer a share of something. But if you want me as a mercenary, I should want paying as well.'

He grinned then.

'That is no problem.'

'You have money?'

'Plenty. You need not worry over that.'

'So you're paying these men of yours, not just promising a share later?'

'I pay, yes.'

I knew too many stories of adventurers who go for buried treasure and on the finding, kill each other to save having to share. It is not so much a plot, perhaps, as a fact of human nature.

The other fact bearing on it is that each man believes It Cannot Happen to Him. That is why he fights. That is why so many die with a look of utter astonishment on their faces. I had seen that look on several occasions.

But if Ferdi was employing a gang of criminal shot firers (mining and general sense) and paying them liberally, the chances of that well-known final scene grew less.

'What do you pay?' I said.

He shrugged.

'What you want. Say.'

'You must have a lot to spare?'

'There is a lot to come.'

'You are very free to speak about it. Suppose that this treasure was in jewels — '

'It is. And others.'

'Other what?'

'Other works of art.'

'I begin to smell out a horde hidden away by the Germans towards the end of the war.'

'You are very clever with your scents.' He laughed briefly.

'So that's it,' I said. 'And you are not merely the seeker, but an agent who has the market ready so that the stuff can be turned into cash.'

'Astute. Yes.'

This explained exactly the hold he had on his men. They were paid, but when it came to the final share out, only Ferdi could sell the stuff. Any of the others trying to do it would be chopped by Interpol almost by return of post.

They were paid; they had a big share to come, and they couldn't do without him.

All this also explained his somewhat timorous efforts as an adventurer. It was money and not courage that drew him into danger.

'You consider?' he said.

'I'm considering, yes.'

What I was considering was how that lunatic girl could think that she alone, having got the map by some trickery, could succeed in finding the long lost hoard entirely on her own. And knowing that others were after it.

'Is that the only map?' I said.

'Yes, as far as is known.'

'You didn't copy it?'

'There was no time. I go to my office with it to put it in the copier, just for a safe copy. The phone goes in my office. I go in a moment. The map is in the copier you understand. Thirty seconds. When I come back — ' He waved his hands.

'Your secretary?'

'Yes.'

'You have an English secretary?'

'To deal with Americans. Yes.'

'You didn't have her long?'

'Three months only.'

Now this was very interesting. I guessed the secretary must be Girlie's friend, from whom she had bought the map, and to see which she had come from home.

Did Girlie know beforehand about the map?

'I think the map's a fake,' I said.

He started and glared at me.

'Impossible!' he said. 'You do not have fake maps made of that — parchment.'

'That is a point. It isn't easily obtainable, though there is such a lot of it about. Where did you get it?'

Another shrug.

'There are still ex-members of the old Nazi régime about, lying low. But it is so long, you know, and the big Chief who had salted away a fortune somewhere in the war is losing his interest. He was fifty then, but he is an old man now. Suddenly, you see, the last few remaining years become more precious than the dream of finding wealth. Perhaps there is no wealth like life when you know there is so little left. Perhaps a man becomes more frightened of losing his life when there is little left than is a young man who thinks he has a lot.'

'Very philosophical,' I said. 'What you really mean is that the older the man got, the cheaper the map became.'

'That is a side effect, yes.'

'And both you and Girlie think the

map refers to this little area of the mountains.'

'On the other side of these hills — ' he waved a hand up at the towering crags, ' — France.'

'Yes, I see.' I threw my cigarette away. 'And did the man — the seller, indicate this part?'

'He did not speak. As soon as I met him, he fell dead.'

Ferdi looked bland and sad.

'You shot the poor devil,' I said. 'When he came to the meeting place you stepped up behind him, and you said, 'Just look ahead and say if you have the map'. When he nodded you shot him in the back.'

Ferdi stared, but his eyes were narrowing all the time. Then he looked away and shrugged.

'As you say. I do not remember.'

'I don't want to have to watch my back all the time,' I said.

'There is no fear. I need a man like you.'

'There is one point. You haven't got the map.'

'The girl cannot stay alone in here for

long. She would go mad.'

'But she knows it. Places are not so frightening when you know them.'

'She will come out in the quarry back there. Paul is waiting in the bush. I expect that is what will happen.'

'Supposing it doesn't?'

'She must. She cannot go on alone.'

'She would be crackers to try. But suppose she doesn't mean to? You wouldn't be surprised to find rivals in the game. Suppose she's selling to them?'

He watched me very carefully then. Obviously this possibility had not occurred to him. He had looked on her as a high pitched eccentric without any real aim but kicks.

Suddenly he'd got a different slant and it dug into him.

'Who would she know?' he snapped.

'The sort of life she's been playing about with — almost anybody. You tried to make contact with her. Why not others?'

'I have seen nobody!'

'That proves nothing.'

'They could not get here. We have the road.'

'I keep suggesting — there may be another.'

'I tell you no!'

'Then how did von Anonymous get a truckload of art treasures from France without another road?'

'The road through the village was there,' he said.

I had forgotten that item. Of course. The village must be on the border, and at night, who would notice just a truck? The Germans had ways of persuading villagers not to see what was inconvenient, either by force or gifts.

As such gifts always belonged to somebody else generosity could be copious.

And then Ferdi changed the subject.

'Let us find the girl. We have agreed. You can go ahead now.'

'We didn't say the figure.'

'State the figure.'

'Ten thousand pounds.'

He looked at me searchingly but said nothing.

'I must have a lot for I have plenty. It must be worth while.'

I reckoned that the more I asked the clearer his situation would become.

'I don't know you that well,' he said.

'I don't know you, either. That's the price. Can you pay it?'

'Of course I can pay it!' he shouted so that his voice echoed down the valley and up into the mountains. It seemed to sober him for he looked around as if the mighty peaks humbled him. 'I must fetch it, though.'

'When? How?'

'I can do it now.'

'If I trust you to go.'

'That is so. But I have said my word.'

'No, I don't think that's enough. I'll come with you to collect. How's that?'

'Okay. Let's find — '

Another noise came from the old door as if somebody had dropped a fair-sized stone near it. We both turned and looked.

A stone, the size of a cricket ball was still moving, rocking on its uneven base. It stopped as we looked.

I ran my eyes up the uneven, rocky face of the cliff above it, but there was no one up there, and it was unlikely that anyone bar an expert rock climber could be up there.

'She is in there!' he snapped, and turned to run.

I grabbed his arm, locked it and turned him back.

'You're still my prisoner until you have the money,' I said.

He glared at me.

'She is there!' he shouted.

'We didn't pass her,' I said again. 'I have told you why I know. Scent clings when a girl hangs about. When she runs, it flees behind her and is swallowed in the air.'

'Who threw that stone?' he countered.

'It fell,' I said, looking up again.

An uncomfortable feeling was coming into the back of my mind that all was not well. But I am not a man of the mountains so I didn't place it. I just instinctively wanted to stay where I was until I could work it out.

'There could be animals up there,' I said.

'I tell you what we do. Go back. Wait. She is sure to come out.'

I looked up the cliff again. A few more pebbles came tumbling down, racing and bumping over the rocky ledges, pattering on to the tram track and bouncing up and over to go spinning down three hundred feet into the trees down in the valley.

'Somebody's up there!' he cried out. 'Up there! On top!'

'Then why doesn't he throw big ones?' I said.

'It is to frighten us. Let us go back. Now!'

'What's the good? Without the girl? If there's somebody watching this ledge, they're looking for her — not us. She's got the map. Better remember that!'

'They can see — '

'They might see but not hit us. We're under an overhang. Look up.'

He looked up. So did I. The small stones and dust and pebbles were coming down faster in a kind of rain. This could not be anybody pushing them over. It was almost a stream.

And then I remembered the village, sawn in half and murdered by the falling rocks of an avalanche.

5

Suddenly the sound of distant water was lost in the quick, hissing rattle of the shower of small stones coming down on to the ledge where we stood. Above us was an overhang of rock, but in an avalanche anything can happen.

The main shower seemed to be on our right, that is between us and our escape door, by which we had come in. To the left there was comparatively little of the now increasing fall of stones.

Amongst the small stones bigger ones began to thud down bounding and cracking down the cliff face. Soon bigger ones still would come.

Even as we stood there against the rock wall, something hit the overhang right above our heads.

A boulder bounced off it and went out and down into the valley. Where it had struck, a crack appeared in the rock underside of the overhang.

'Run!' I said. 'That way!'

We ran, skidding and tripping on the moving carpet of small stones raining down. I kept my hands clasped over my head and several times sharp blows shocked up my arms from the hail of stones.

A boulder came down in the middle of the shower. It missed Ferdi as he ran madly for the tunnel mouth, but it hit the ground ahead of me, and I went headlong over it before it rolled on over the rim of the ledge.

Stones rained on me, hurting in a hundred places at once as I scrambled up and went on, stumbling worse now from pain and a kind of dizziness brought on by the intensity of the murderous shower.

From behind me I heard and felt the thump and shiver of the big rocks coming down. The sound of the avalanche had become a roar and the rock ledge was trembling under the onslaught.

Ferdi had got into the tunnel. As I ran to join him a great fissure appeared in the rock ledge between the tracks of the old tramway dead ahead of me.

I twisted and jumped sideways up against the rock wall, still six feet from the safety of the tunnel. The crack opened wider and came in diagonally to the wall. It opened up, putting a gulf between me and my goal.

There was one way only, to jump from a narrowing foothold across a widening crack, one growing so fast that it appeared the whole ground was slipping away down the cliff into the valley.

In the storm of stones and fear I couldn't see that it was the part I stood on that was falling away.

As I jumped my footing slid away under me and my spring lost half its power. Instead of clearing the gap horizontally I suddenly found myself jumping below the level of the ledge I had to reach.

I got the edge of it with my hands and just hung there while the remainder of the ledge I had stood on roared away below me. For a few seconds I just hung there, my head against the rough rock, stones beating on my shoulders and back and sometimes hitting my fingers as I hung on. It was like somebody trying to hammer me loose.

Well practised in the art of gymnastics, and fit as I was, I just couldn't haul myself up for those first few seconds. The din, the constant hammering of stones confused and weakened me.

The thought flashed into my head that perhaps Ferdi would see and come to help. Common sense was still in my head, however, and I realised that it would well suit him to let me go down with the rocks.

I hauled myself up until my chin was level with the ledge. A rock of some size struck my right shoulder and I went down again, my right side paralysed for the moment.

After that I was practically hanging by one hand for I could feel nothing of my right one.

It seemed to me then but a matter of a few seconds more before I got smashed off my hold or had to let go.

I made a desperate effort to pull up, but my right arm had no power. I looked up. The edge of the rock floor seemed to be drawing further away, upwards, as if my hands were coming loose.

Then the girl's face appeared there. There was no time to feel surprised. She dropped a rope over.

'Hang on. It's fixed,' she said, and vanished.

The rope fell over my shoulder. I was being saved, but only one hand had feeling and that had to hold the rock. The other couldn't grasp the rope at all because the fingers had nothing but numbness.

The rope was over my back and it was obviously then the only hope of life.

I pulled the numbed hand from the ledge and hung with one only. Then I twisted myself against the rock, left side into it and hunched my right shoulder as best I could.

For a moment the rope hung at my back still. I wriggled and almost lost my grip, but it worked. The rope slid round my shoulder and came to my front. I got it with my legs, rope climber fashion. My grip was enough to hold me while I shifted my left hand from the rock and gripped the rope.

I fell. For a moment I thought she had tricked me, but after a fall of a foot, the rope tautened and then held me. I hung there slowly turning and bumping against the rock.

The stone storm eased slightly and seemed to be falling further out from me, as if coming down at greater speed from above which threw the fall outwards.

The rope began to jerk, then to pull upwards slowly.

I shifted my grip before my fist was pulled over the sharp rock edge and got hold of the horizontal part above. I was being pulled up steadily, strongly.

My body was heaved over the edge on to the tracks again and I went slithering over the loose stones, dragged on almost to the tunnel before I let go.

When I got to my feet, she was inside the tunnel standing by an old winch, round the winder of which she had wound the rope.

'Excellent girl,' I said, feeling my shoulder.

'You want to take more care,' she said.

She was filthy with stone dust and rust and black from the winding engine. It made her look saucier than ever.

'I didn't expect to see you so soon,' I said.

'Ferdi said you'd gone down with the avalanche.'

'He would. Where is he?'

'In the tunnel. Smoking. He's got the shakes.'

'So have I,' I said.

'You don't look it. You just look dirty.'

'I'll lend you a mirror.'

In the emotional reaction of the moment I wished I didn't know her father so well.

'Why did you run off?' I asked.

'I get spasms,' she said. 'I just have to run. That's all.'

'Why don't you ever tell the truth?'

'It's a bore. Ask my political papa. He should know.'

'Stack it. You've been here before. You know the place. How much do you know? Is the valley on the map the one down there?'

'What a wild guess.'

'Make it wilder. Say.'

'I don't know but it could be.'

'Did you make that dash on a hunch, or did you know the valley was here?'

'Somebody told me it might be.'

'Your friend? Ferdi's English secretary?'

'You do ask a lot of questions.'

'How did she know? Ferdi didn't.'

'She must have talked to somebody.'

I changed the subject.

'What do you intend to do when you've found this little lot?'

She smiled.

'Spend it,' she said.

'How will you get it away?'

'Helicopter, I suppose. I hadn't really thought.' I switched again.

'Did you find anything just now?'

'No.'

'Show me where you went.'

'Oh, I couldn't remember.'

'I'll help you. Start along the tunnel.'

'I don't think I went there.'

'In view of the fact that the connecting ledge fell away before you found me, there is nowhere else you could have gone.'

'You're too logical for me.'

'For God's sake stop messing about!'

'Don't lose your temper, darling. We won't get anything done that way.'

'I'm very grateful to you for saving my life, but I won't stand much more of this butterfly stuff. Show me where you went.'

'But Ferdi would see.'

'Ferdi can't do anything. His men are on the other side of that fall. He won't act on his own.'

'Well, if he's all alone, won't he be a bit like a rat in the corner?'

'I'll risk it. Show me where you went.'

She sighed and turned away.

'You're horrid.'

I pushed her in the back to start her off. Then she went on, quickly, almost breaking into a run.

'Not that again,' I said.

She slowed. I saw her shoulders shake as if she laughed.

The daylight faded. I used my light again. We didn't see Ferdi.

She walked on quickly, wiggling her bottom enthusiastically. She didn't seem to need my light, but as I was to learn she had a fantastic photographic memory for places.

Once she had seen a place, anywhere, she could walk through it accurately, blindfold practically.

She kept on at a cracking pace through the darkness, blotting out most of my light with her own dancing shadow.

We came to a crossroads of tunnels. She swung to the right one and went marching on. I stopped her then.

'When did you see Ferdi last?' I said.

She looked round at me.

'Way back there,' she said. 'Smoking, he was, like I said in my tiny accurate way.'

'He's moved on since,' I said. 'He didn't have a light, either.'

'I didn't see him lying down anywhere.'

'He must have taken one of these tunnels. In the pitch dark. He was much too frightened a man to do that on his own.'

'How can you be so sure?'

'He's scared of the dark. I had enough proof of that way back.'

'Then where is he?' Her voice was

quicker, sharper as if this phenomenon had roused her keenest interest.

'That's what I'm trying to find out. He went into the dark. He had no light. Yet he was scared to death of the dark.'

'Then why did he go?'

'He was forced.'

Now she stopped and her staring eyes were bright in the backglare of my little lamp.

'There's nobody here to force but us chickens,' she said. There was an uneasy note in her voice.

I felt uneasy, too. That could be the only explanation of Ferdi going into the dark. But who had forced? How did anyone else come to be this side of the fallen ledge?

★   ★   ★

We had to find him and see what was happening. We went back and down two of the tunnels before we came upon him.

He was lying between the tram tracks, slightly huddled, flat out and with blood coming from his head.

110

We had a look at him. It looked as if he had been slugged from behind, and the way he was lying suggested he was being forced deeper into the tunnel when the blow had fallen.

'Is he bad?' she said.

'Don't know. The skin's broken but I can't tell if his skull's cracked.'

We stayed still, listening. Some water plashed a long way off, but that was all. The roar of the avalanche had either stopped or been smothered by the tunnel acoustics. I shone the light all ways. Nothing. Nobody.

'Why do it?' she said.

'It gets him out of the way, doesn't it?'

'Will he die?'

'Eventually. Not from this.'

I used his handkerchief and some of his shirt to bind him up.

'He's hiding. The assassin,' she said.

'Seems to show there's only one of him.'

I picked Ferdi up fireman fashion and carried him back to the crossroad. I laid him down there with his jacket for a pillow and left him.

'Go on where you left off,' I said.

We walked on again, our footfalls echoing.

'What do you expect?' she said.

'Anything — from you.'

She laughed.

'That's what you'll get.'

We went on. Once more we came to a door, but this time the tram tracks went under it, so the door ended four inches above the ground.

She turned to me and smiled slowly.

'The other side you have to walk steady,' she said. 'It's just a plank.'

'I can get used to planks,' I said, lifted the bar and groaned the door open.

The light showed a vast mass of black nothing with just a narrow plank running across it. It looked like the last bridge across the Styx.

'What is this?' I said.

'What is this?' My own voice came back, echoing in a space so vast that it kept on, getting smaller, smaller, whispering in the emptiness and finally dying out. It seemed the echo lasted seconds.

'It's a big place,' she said.

I pointed the torch down over the broken edge of the floor; I saw the twisted ends of the rails where they had been torn off by the earth falling from under them. They twisted in the air like petrified worms.

The light showed nothing else. Whatever was below was too far down for the torch to reach.

And there was just this narrow plank across it.

I looked back.

'What's the matter?' she said quickly.

'There is someone besides us in this place,' I said. 'It wouldn't be too well if he came up behind while we were on that plank. Is there a bar on the other side of the door?'

She felt round it while I shone the torch back along the tunnel.

'Yes. But if the door's shut there won't be room to stand the other side.'

'Thoughtless,' I said. 'Did you cross this in the dark?' I was incredulous of her careless courage.

'Turn the light out,' she said.

I did. After a few seconds the plank

glowed a faint green in the blackness.

'It's not so scary, walking it like that,' she said. 'You can't see there's nothing underneath like you can with a light.' She laughed a moment. 'Besides, I had the gun to hold as a balance pole.'

Looking at the thin green line suspended in nothing it was impossible to gauge whether it ran for ten yards or a hundred.

'This must have been part of the safety devices,' I said. 'People don't like crossing planks hundreds of feet up. What's below, I wonder? A pool full of alligators?'

'I don't want to know,' she said. 'What do we do?'

'Go on. What else? But be careful. I'll watch the rear end.'

'Watch your step, too,' she said.

'I'll do that. Go on.'

We started off. The plank was as wide as my foot only, but it was steel. Turning to look back needed concentration, but I kept doing it to make sure.

We didn't use the light. As she said, it was easier to walk the illuminated line than to use a light and bring it sharply out of focus for want of a background.

For the second time the task of walking slowly in pitch dark made it difficult to estimate distance travelled. More, after a while I began to get a sharp impression that I was walking steeply uphill. It was like flying at night and suddenly getting the wind up so that you began to think your instruments are all wrong.

Give way to that little spasm, and you're dead before you have time to sort things out.

This was the same. Perhaps it was turning to peer in the blackness behind us. Perhaps it was just sheer funk. Either way it was happening.

'How much longer?' I said, feeling sweat break out and freeze on my face.

'It's a way yet.'

I closed my eyes a moment to steady myself, then looked back.

Naturally I thought I saw something move back there in the black space. The sweat got colder still. I strained my eyes to see, but all there was to see was the thin ribbon of the long steel joist we walked on.

'Is it all right?' she said.

No matter how quietly we spoke the echoes whispered back a thousand times.

'I can't see anything,' I said.

She had stopped and I felt her against me. I also felt my feet were beginning to swing up above my head, as I floated around in the vastness of space.

'Go on,' I whispered.

It was better moving. The concentration of placing the feet and keeping balance eased the tendency to hallucinations.

Once again I looked back, and once more thought I saw something move at the end of the green strip.

Another hallucination. Or was somebody really there, letting us lead him to a place of which he had no real knowledge?

If that was the case we were safe for a while. He could have fired without seeing us; just fired along the green strip and four feet above it. He would have been bound to hit me.

But if he wanted us to lead him to the treasure, we were safe yet.

We went on. I couldn't see the strip

116

ahead because of her body, but suddenly she gave a little gasp.

'What is it?' I said, alarmed.

'The end,' she said and laughed breathlessly. 'Solid ground. Feel.'

I felt her hand groping for mine and used the torch at last. We had reached another tunnel, perhaps one that had originally joined with the one we had left before the inside of the mountain had collapsed.

'Kicky, wasn't it?' she said.

'Like mad,' I agreed and wiped my face.

Standing on the rock helped the hallucination to go away. I shone the light back along the joist. It seemed endless. The light didn't reach the door we had left, but ended in a mist, as if the darkness just mopped it up.

'You think there's somebody?' she whispered.

'I keep getting the feeling.'

'So do I.'

'It could be just a mirage from wind-up. Let's get on.'

'We're nearly there,' she said.

We went on along a tunnel and a light began to appear ahead. It wasn't daylight. More like a glow through an aquarium tank. It didn't get brighter, but spread more, softly making gloom of the darkness.

'We're there,' she said.

Suddenly the tunnel widened out into a wide, low cave, lit by this odd greenish light by which we saw the treasure at last.

It was incredible. True, there were numbers of crates and cases and tea chests standing around, but standing, leaning, parked around in heavy gilt frames were garish posters advertising the joys and delights, the strength and vengeance of the Nazi régime.

The lurid colours in the green light made them look like something putrefying. They were fantastic, bloody, belligerent, nightmarish, exalting blood, slaughter and war and cursing the British, the Americans and particularly the Russians.

I had seen many reproductions of old Nazi posters, but never anything like these. They seemed to be hell's caricatures of posters, a madman's slashing, a

massed bad dream of propagandic phan-
tasmagoria.

'Well?' she said, and laughed.

'My God!' I said. 'Is this what
everybody came for? In gilt frames!'

I started looking in the nearest crates
and chests. More of these monstrosities.
A lunatic's collection.

I sat down on a chest and looked at
her.

'Of course, nothing is valueless in these
days of crazes,' I said. 'But what an earth
is this worth? Who collects this junk?'

'They're originals,' she said.

'Very original. I should think even
Hitler would have been shaken by this
lot.'

She sat down on the chest beside me.

'It's a bit of a shock at first, isn't it? But
there's more. In those boxes over there,
busts of Germania, and when I say bust I
mean bust. Scale models of Hitler and
Goering, all in porcelain, and all as bad as
this.'

'It's so mad there's obviously something more,' I said. 'Obviously.'

'Somebody always loves somebody

somewhere,' she said. 'There's a market for everything.'

'But you? Why did you — ?'

'I didn't know this was what it was till just now. That's why I came back to find you.'

Movement above made me look up sharply. It was a fish, whirling and twisting on the ceiling. My aquarium likeness had not been so far out. The ceiling was some kind of very thick green glass fixed in round holes cut in the rock. It could have been part of the old mine, perhaps put in before the lake had formed up above it.

Surely it couldn't have been engineered purposely to hold this collection of jimjam ware?

We got up and went along the cavern to another leading off it. Still more of the lewd junk. The busts were, as she had said, grotesque with swastikas for nipples. There were some three-quarter length statues of Germanic ladies, big bosomed, all pregnant and with swastika navels, no doubt indicating the incipient birth of noble soldiers.

'This is awful,' I said. 'Somebody must have worked like mad to create these monstrosities. One of the great mysteries of human nature is how someone can be so bad and believe he's good. Isn't there anything but this pornography?'

She gripped my wrist and raised the rifle slightly in the other hand.

'There's someone in the other cave,' she whispered.

She let me go. I went to the opening, kept to the side and peered round into the larger cave. I didn't see anything move but a fish in one of the ceiling portholes. It distracted, for the light was not all that good, and in half-light one tends to imagine movement when strained.

The surprise of the cave contents had taken my mind off watch. I suppose in that hall of unreality everything took on the unreal.

Standing still there and watching the other hall, I felt the aches and bruises of my body begin to nag and burn. I must have been drifting a bit, not concentrating so that I didn't feel much. Yogi notion.

Pain makes one impatient. It made me.

I stayed a while and saw nothing, so I went out, gun in hand, and walked about amongst the piles of cases and crazy pictures, pushing things with my foot when I thought it could hide somebody.

When I came to the end and found nobody, I was angry and disappointed.

'There's nothing here,' I called back.

'Oh.'

That was all. A small sound, and one that made me instantly distrustful. She was such a baggage of apparently irrelevant tricks, anything could count.

She didn't come out into the larger cave. I went back in to get her and couldn't find her.

'Where the hell are you?' I said.

No answer. With that I got furious. I went round the cave, which was far bigger than I had thought, and full of niches, crevices, cracks, holes, even pits down near the farthest walls.

It was rather like the side of a big cheese, when I began to look round. What I was looking for was a place that she could have got out through in another of her eccentric flights.

I couldn't find one, but it was difficult to be sure. Some of the niches were cracked right in, crooked as flattened out corkscrews. Some of the crates, too, were jammed up against the walls so that they could have hidden holes.

At the end of the first angry time round I wasn't sure I had looked everywhere possible.

I called her again and thought she might have got out into the larger cave without me seeing her, for I hadn't been sure she had called out 'Oh' from there; just assumed it.

Back there I couldn't find her either.

By this time I was aching all over and fuming as well. Not the best state for thinking, and what I needed to do then was think.

The best I could do was think there must be some kind of a crack out from a hole, niche, cranny or jink, so I went back and started to search them all again.

My head was thumping from the pain in my shoulder, which had now pro-claimed itself king of all the rest of the bruises, and when I bent it got worse.

But I went round the ragged walls a second time and still found nothing.

Again I called. No answer. She must be fooling again on one of her impulse flights.

As I went to go back into the larger cave I saw a foot sticking up out of a case of Germanian maidens. One thing I had noticed, that none of these effigies had any feet.

This was a real one.

And it didn't move.

6

The surprise had something comic about it, even in that atmosphere. One solitary booted female foot sticking up out of a crate was part of a comedy.

I ran to the case and looked in. She was head-first into a gaggle of porcelain busts, some of which even seemed to have a look of surprise on their gaudy faces.

She was quite flaccid when I heaved her out and laid her on the floor. I couldn't make out what was the matter with her for I could see no sign of injury. I had the instinct to try slapping her face to test for shamming, but she seemed really out, her head rolling like a doll's.

There was dead silence all round. The only movement was of the fish swirling in the roof panels of the next cave. I thought she might have fainted from lack of food or too much excitement, or heat, but none fitted her lively personality at all. I couldn't really think of her fainting for lack of food. She would sit down long before that happened and start giving orders for her escort to start hunting.

So it came back to some kind of knockout drop. But who and how? And where was the giver?

I left her lying where I could see her and made another sweep of the two caves. But the heaped up boxes and the high gilt frames made it an excellent scene for hide and seek. Any sneaker could watch where I went and just slip round one heap or another so that he was always on the blind side.

Then I heard her call.

'What the devil happened?'

I ran back. She was sitting up and shaking her head.

'Somebody hit me,' she said, and rubbed her poll.

'I couldn't find anything,' I said. 'Not that I'm an expert skull pusher, but I couldn't find a bump.'

'No,' she said, and stared. 'No. It's inside, now I begin to come to. Inside. I've got a hangover. Boy! It's clanging now!'

She held her head but at the front this time. The delayed kick was on. It meant knockout drops all right. This was exactly the programme.

'You didn't eat anything? Take a drink? Smoke?' I said.

'I don't remember,' she said blankly. 'No, I couldn't, could I? I haven't a light, there's no water I can see. Got nothing to eat, either.'

'Not a sweet you had in your pocket?'

'I didn't have any.'

'Did you smell anything?' I said hopefully.

'Nothing more than the pong of old wooden crates and straw and the rest of it. No. Nothing out of the way.'

'You were upside down in that crate,' I said.

'What? Me? I hope you didn't look.'

'Of course not. I shut my eyes and hauled you out.'

'I must have looked sordid.'

'No. Just ridiculous.'

'You're one of the most complimentary bastards I ever — '

'Shut up and think. Did you smell

anything? Have you got any smell in your subconscious? Think of yourself as standing on your head again and see if it recalls any smell.'

She tried. She shut her eyes and held her hands to her head to ease the clanging.

'You're clever,' she said, suddenly looking up. 'A musty smell. Yes.'

'Where? Suddenly under your nose?'

I was keeping a close watch all round, but only the fish moved beyond ourselves.

'No. In the crate. I bent to look in the crate. That was it. And that was all. Out like a light. I didn't even notice myself going. Just out. Switched off!'

I went to the crate again and looked in at the gathering of shiny busts. The top edges of the crate were wood outer skin with an inch square brace all along the inside, forming a lip all round. There was a crack between the outer skin and the brace.

'Did you grip the edge of this box?' I said.

'I suppose I did, because I was reaching down in there to get one of those Gerties up.'

She got to her feet and came to me at the crate.

'I think,' I said, 'that if you grip this edge, the two pieces of wood squeeze together and release some knockout gas. Stand right back and hold your breath.'

I stood at arm's length, stopped breathing and squeezed the crack between the wood tight shut. It closed easily and a small puff of vapour rose up from it, spreading quickly in the air.

'Back out of it!' I said and jumped back and she went even further in retreat.

'Well, well,' she said, startled. 'After all these years, and still working!'

'Dragon, guardian of the cave,' I said, and when it had cleared I went back.

Very careful now, I pushed a smaller box up, stood on it and reached down into the porcelain group of maidens. I got one and lifted it out gingerly.

'Stand well to the rear,' I said.

She stepped back and I hurled the maiden at the rock wall ten feet away. The maiden burst into a thousand pieces and crashed to the ground in a storm of china.

That was all. We went over and searched the pieces, but there was nothing but the broken pieces.

'But that gas guarded something,' I said. 'Let's try some more.'

Another one produced the same result, just adding to the debris on the floor.

When the third burst, it looked different. It was a different kind of explosion.

We jumped on the largest piece. It was a maiden's breast with a swastika nipple, but on the inside, which was almost solid, what looked like diamonds had been baked into the china.

'Treasure!' she gasped.

I went to break it up against the wall but saw the powdered pieces lying amongst the broken china on the floor. They had broken quite differently. There was a lot of powder down there now.

I rubbed the inside of the breast with my thumb.

'Chalk,' I said. 'The stuff they make cheap statuettes of. Well, well.'

'Get it out. Quickly. I'm agasp!'

I got my penknife and started to dig

away the chalky stuff. The breast was full of diamonds, matching in diminishing sizes from a really big to a peasize. I put them into her cupped hands as I got them out.

'The secret of the grim masks is solved,' I said. 'Perhaps the paintings cover other paintings. That has been done before.'

'See if there's any more,' she said eagerly, and stuffed the stones into her trouser pocket as if they had been pebbles, perhaps so I shouldn't take much notice. I got on the box again and handed her out bust after bust. She set them on the ground as she got them.

'We'll scratch 'em,' I said. 'That's the quickest. The china ones won't mark, the chalk ones will.'

I went along a line of fifteen just scratching once. Two were marked. I slung them at the wall. More diamonds.

'I wondered why they were all pregnant,' she said, giggling from sheer excitement.

I filled her hands again and she watched with bright, almost lustful eyes.

'Golly! And look at all the other crates!' she breathed. 'Come on! Break some more!'

'That's enough to prove our point,' I said.

She looked up sharply.

'What do you mean?'

'Use your head. I want none of this stuff, nor do you. It's a truckload of murder motive once you know what's behind the hideous mask.'

'What are you going to do, then?'

'Get you out of this bloody place. What do you think?'

'What about all this?'

'Give it up. Tell somebody. Save a few lives.'

'You're bonkers!' she said incredulously.

'Think seriously for a moment. This is Spain. You've found treasure trove. Stolen by Germans now dead, from people who could be deader, having been gone much longer. So whose? The Spanish Government will lay claim. You've already said how they chuck you into jug at the toss of a coin. If they thought you'd stolen this, what do you think would happen to you?'

'Yes, but there must be a way. There's a way over from France — '

'Isn't that just as impossible? What will you do with it, supposing you can get it into a suitcase — just enough to suit your greedy mind? Hasn't it occurred to you that this stuff is unmanageable?'

'But Ferdi was going to — '

'Ferdi is a market operative. He knows how to deal with it. He has his channels all ready for the deals. You've got nothing at all.'

She had her right hand in her pocket, which was now stuffed with diamonds.

'Keep the pocketful,' I said. 'Nobody'll miss them. But you'll have one hell of a job to smuggle even that lot. The best you can do is sell 'em to Ferdi.'

'He'd diddle me,' she said indignantly.

'Heavens!' I said. 'Your morality staggers me.'

'Well, he would.'

'Let's see,' I said. 'But meanwhile, we must find a way out before we starve here. In your excitement you may have forgotten that our way back has gone in an avalanche.'

Momentarily, the treasure took second place. She even seemed quick enough to be badly frightened.

'There couldn't just have been one way in,' she said.

'One way would explain that carefully contrived tight walk,' I said. 'It means going back over it.'

'How did they get all this here, then?'

'There's an old military dodge of getting guns across rivers. You sling a cable across, run a pulley on it with a large net hanging from the hook on it. The net is full of gun. I'd guess that way.'

'Then it would be easy — ' she started.

'Forget it, you little moron!' I said, losing my temper.

'Anybody'd think you didn't want to find it!'

'I'm not wasting time arguing with a child. Come on out of here.'

She pouted, looked very sulky and angry, then went by me into the larger cave. I should have suspected this instant agreement, but I was tired and hurting all over and just impatient to find a way out now that the secret was open.

I had seen something stranger than I'd ever seen before, but its attraction for me was in the grisly, grand guignol type of the presentation. The value involved was to me a snare.

'It's just because you don't need money!' she snapped out, turning round suddenly.

'Nor do you,' I said. 'You have a successful father.'

'Successful. Maybe. But he keeps two women, and he keeps them high. Mother asks for more because she knows about Freda, and Freda wants more because she's taking the risk, and I tell you, there isn't much spills over.'

'You've got a pocketful of loot,' I said. 'Now get on.'

I pushed her. She stuck her tongue out, then whirled round in a temper and marched on out of the cave.

My idea wasn't to let her get pinched with that load of stuff on her but to ease it off her once I had persuaded her out of this mountain catacomb.

But sometimes things change one's mind. She did.

I didn't use the torch out to the edge of the tightwalk but let the long stretch gleam in the darkness. It was easier on the eyes and it didn't show anything across the chasm.

I had told her to keep dead quiet and on the edge of that doomy walk she seemed frightened enough to comply.

We waited a minute or two to get our eyes dead set into the conditions, and then I was about to urge her forward when I noticed something odd.

The long green line, stretching into the distance was shortening.

I gripped her arm tightly for dead silence, and strained my eyes to see the green line and make sure it was not my sight that was playing against me.

But no. The line was growing shorter, as if the long beam was being pulled in under the ledge on which we stood.

The feeling it gave was uncanny and terrifying. She drew in a short, quick breath and for an instant I feared another scream. But she stayed dead quiet, and still save from a slight trembling which I could feel running in her body.

Then my vision caught up on my twisted mind and I saw the scene the other way round. It was not the beam shortening under us, but the glow being obliterated by someone creeping along it, blocking the glow behind by the shadow of his body.

When I realised it I moved. I moved her gently by my hands so that she came round to the back of me. By then I think she realised what was going on.

The approaching shadow came very slowly, but as I knew, that stretch was no place for a fast walk. I got the pistol from my pocket and thumbed up the safety trip.

He made no sound that I could hear until there seemed only about ten feet of luminous strip left. Then I heard soft, but very quick breathing.

I felt her press against me as if for comfort in the tension and I reached round and eased her back from me. I didn't want her jamming my action.

It had mesmeric effect, watching the

strip shortening. The thing was I had to let him get a footing on the ledge. To scare him off the beam would be to lose him somewhere in the pit below and I couldn't take the risk of killing someone who might know the way out.

For a moment I wondered if it could be Ferdi recovered, but dismissed that possibility. Ferdi, afraid of the dark, and suffering the hangover of a head blow, certainly wouldn't have tried a trip like this one.

It left the three of Ferdi's team. The two truckmen, whom I couldn't imagine making a silent journey, and the man who had been with Ferdi in the car.

The line shortened. I could hear his breathing plainly, and he was a tense man. I could hear that, too.

With two feet to go the movement ceased. I heard the man gasp, and instinctively I knew what was happening. The idea of the tension being nearly over had screwed him up and let him go. He was swaying on the beam.

I reached out and grabbed an arm. It was waving in the air, trying to claw a balance out of nothing.

'Himmel!' the cry rose up and echoed in the place.

Suddenly the full weight of a falling body came on my left arm. I let it go a moment then twisted so that the man's weight was slung in towards the ledge. He thudded on the rock, thumped like a kicked football, and then he clutched my arm with both hands to haul himself up.

'Steady, you fool!' I shouted. 'We'll both go!'

He was pulling me headlong into the darkness, and I could not let go.

'No, no!' the girl screamed out from behind me and then her arms wrapped round my waist and she pulled back so that the breath was almost squeezed out of me.

How long that threesome tug-of-war went on I shudder to think now. He seemed to be hanging over the ledge. Her pulling back had saved my balance and after we had steadied a bit under the man's weight, I got a sound footing and started to pull back until I heard his feet scrabbling to get a hold on the rock.

He was panting hard with fear and the effort. She was pulling and gasping in my ear.

'Hold it!' I remember getting breath enough to get it out. 'Hold it! Now — together — heave!'

She did it wrong. We didn't get anywhere. By then my arm seemed to be pulled out of the socket. I called again and this time we got it together.

We heaved strongly. I felt my shoulder crack, but the man was using more sense now and held my hand with only one of his own and grabbed the rock with the other. There was a lot of scratching and gasping and then he was on dry land.

He let go. My arm almost flew up and off its bearings, the reaction was so great. She started to laugh breathlessly behind me.

'Never a dull moment,' she gasped.

I forced my left hand into my pocket, brought the torch out and switched it on. It blazed like fire and I'd forgotten to close my eyes to start with. But as my sight cleared I saw a dark young man crouched on the ledge by my feet, face down, gasping.

He looked up, his face running with sweat. I did not know him at all.

He didn't say anything. Slowly, by stages he rolled over, sat up, did some breathing exercises to steady himself, then helping himself with one hand on the rock tunnel wall he got to his feet. He was bigger than he had looked crouching on the ground.

He didn't thank anybody. He just grinned.

'Who are you?' I said.

'Gleist,' he said. It didn't seem enough.

'Are you looking for me?' I said.

'No. The fräulein.' He grinned then, as if his general capacity for insolence had returned from a short absence. 'We are friends.'

'I never saw him before in my life!' the girl protested.

But then she protested such a lot and she lied like the shaking of a bird's feathers, ruffling truth all the time.

The man laughed.

'The fräulein must please herself,' he

said. 'Perhaps she forgets very soon. Perhaps she does not mean to remember. It is nothing to me. We know each other now.'

He laughed then. I saw that he flicked his glance from her to the tunnel.

'Did you meet anyone on the way?' I said.

'A thief,' he said, shrugging. 'It was nothing.'

'Did you lay him with a rock?'

'Some wood,' he said.

'Why do you call him a thief?'

'Is he not? Is that not his business?'

'It's a matter of opinion. I don't know enough about him. I wonder whether you do.'

'Intentions make the crook.'

'How do you know his intentions?'

'He came here to steal. So did the fräulein. Perhaps you, also.'

He looked sneering, his voice sharp and cutting.

'You sound as if you have a personal interest in these projected thefts,' I said. Then I took a long shot. 'Wasn't there a General von Gleist in the German Army during the war?'

He grinned again, but didn't bother to answer.

'He's dead,' I said. 'He died a few days ago in Santander.'

His grin got sterner but it stayed on his face long after any humour had left it.

'I had heard,' he said.

Perhaps. But it was obvious he hadn't heard his 'thief' had done the murder. He was clearly some relative, perhaps even a son, and he looked the sort of man to be malicious to a high degree if he had his knife into anyone.

'What have you come for, then?' the girl said.

'The same thing as you,' he said, 'only this happens to be mine.'

'What — all of it?' she said.

'It is not entirely for me,' he said. 'I have many friends.'

There was a menacing note about that remark. Almost as if his friends were somewhere nearby, ready to act.

One of our dangers which had not struck me until that moment was that we knew of the treasure now, so that if anyone wished to seize it and keep it secret — which they would have to — they would have to keep us secret, too.

I decided to try the innocent, for I guessed he knew nothing about me.

'Your suspicions aren't well founded,' I said. 'All we want is to find a way out of this place. If you can show us one, you'll be left in peace with whatever is yours.'

His eyes narrowed in surprise, then glanced quickly at the girl.

'That's true,' she said. 'This place doesn't suit my complexion.'

Gleist's face remained stonily suspicious.

'But you knew the way in,' he said.

'That fell down,' I said. 'It's blocked now. Well? Agreed? You show us, we'll leave you.'

'Suppose I show you and you go and get friends? That would be no bargain.'

'We have no friends here. We're not as lucky as you.'

'And how do I know?'

'You don't know. But if we had they'd be with us now.'

He grinned.

'Please do not think that because mine

are not with me that they are not here.'

'Well, you ask me to believe you on that point. You might as well believe me. You see for yourself, we were on our way back when we met.'

He thought a moment, watching me, then he nodded briefly.

'It is so,' he said. 'But I warn you that if you speak to anyone of this place, you will be killed.'

I agreed to that one, too.

The quiet of the place was somehow gathering an interference difficult to catch and explain. A sound so far off it could not be heard, only felt. That's the only way I could think of it.

We all three looked up into the air, wondering what it was. For a whole minute it stayed, like the ghost of a sound that wouldn't come to life.

'What is that?' Gleist said at last.

He looked taut, as if it might be something of our doing that he couldn't explain.

'The ground's trembling,' the girl said suddenly. 'Feel.'

She bent down and put her hand on the rock. So did I. It could be felt, trembling uneasily, but too slight to be felt through the sole of a shoe.

'Earthquake!' she hissed.

'More like the avalanche, still going on,' I said.

Gleist hadn't bothered to feel the ground. He just stood there, his face shining with sweat.

'How did your way get blocked?' he said.

'Landslide. Feels as if it's still going on, or started again. Once things begin to move, they move other things.'

'Let's find that way out,' the girl said suddenly. 'I don't like this!'

'What's this? Woman's instinct?' I said. 'You can hardly feel it. What makes you think — '

'I've just got the feeling, that's all. Let's find the way out.'

Gleist was staring up into the darkness as if to see the source of the tremble. He wiped his face on his bare forearm and continued to look up. It made me look up, too, but there was only pitch blackness.

'Yes, perhaps the fräulein is wise,' he said huskily. 'There is only this bridge — '

As he spoke there was a sudden increase in the trembling. It became a thundering sound, not loud, but distinct now.

'Let's go!' she cried out, pushing me.

'Don't be a fool! I'm on the edge!' It was my turn to shout.

'Yes. Let us go,' Gleist said, and turned towards the long, narrow beam. 'It will be safer the other side.'

I realised he had nothing to worry over once he was on safe ground. He could come back and sling the cable over and do the gun-across-the-river act to get himself, his friends and the treasure across.

I got hold of the girl and brought her round in front of me.

'You keep in the middle and don't let the noise panic you,' I said.

But I could feel her shivering as she went in front of me. Gleist's face was literally wet with sweat. For myself, the increasing noise was gnawing the very ends of my nerves, so we all felt the same.

The sound was getting louder all the time but it didn't seem to be anywhere inside the cavern. It still seemed far outside the shell of rock we must be inside.

I put the light out. The girl gasped and Gleist swore. We stayed getting used to the dark until we could see the soft green glow of the bridge clearly.

The noise was then getting much louder, but still was outside the cavern.

'I go now,' Gleist said hoarsely.

I heard his voice strained and shaky and hoped he wouldn't lose his balance again. The noise was eating into our nerves anyhow, and that was bound to affect the safety of our crossing.

Then suddenly he called out.

'Himmel! It is shaking right along! It will come loose!'

7

'Come back off it!'

I shouted to Gleist and I needed to. Apart from the sudden trembling of everything around us, the roar of thunder echoed in the huge cavern.

He came off the luminous beam, bumped into the girl and she into me. We stood there, huddled on the edge of an invisible precipice, petrified by a sudden deafening fury of sound.

The girl got me round the waist and clung to me as if I was some rampart that could keep from the coming storm.

'Himmel!' Gleist shouted. 'It is earthquake!'

It could have been. The mountain had been moving that afternoon, the slipping of the small stones starting bigger ones, then rocks, and then anything that was loose or could be cracked and broken loose by the movement of tons of moving stone.

'What is it?' she yelled in my ear.

'God knows. Get back in the tunnel.'

I used my torch then and pulled her into the tunnel mouth. Gleist turned, blinded by the light, and felt his way along the wall, following my shouting. He was panting when we got into the tunnel. The light went out. I shook it, and it flickered. A loose connection somewhere.

In the new darkness we could see the green beam stretching out over the abyss.

'It moves!' Gleist bellowed. 'Look, look!'

The beam seemed to be wandering from side to side. It was difficult to see what caused that illusion until suddenly it began to bend into an arc like a bow. What colossal energy was being applied to that steel joist couldn't be guessed at, but it seemed that the walls of rock must be closing in on each other, bending the girder that joined them.

The arc grew more acute and then something gave, for the beam jumped into the air, quivering, twisted and then plunged down into the darkness.

'We shall not get out now!' Gleist

roared. 'We are lost!'

It didn't need saying. It was too damned obvious, for Gleist who knew this place wouldn't have risked the long cruise along that beam if there had been another way.

'What shall we do?' she screamed.

I could hardly hear her, the world seemed to be breaking up in a ghastly, tearing storm of violent sound. It hurt the eardrums, shook the skin, sickened the bowels. It was terrifying, stunning.

The girl started sobbing against me like a frightened child. I hung on to her as tightly as she hung to me. I heard Gleist gasping somewhere near, as if he cried out loud.

The whole tunnel shook and pieces of stone began to fall from the roof.

'Get back into the cave!' I shouted.

'No!' she screamed. 'That glass — in the roof! If it cracks, the lake — We'll drown!'

I didn't think it was that kind of glass, but with the mighty movement of the angry mountain, any sort of armoured glass might be shattered, as the steel beam had been twisted and thrown away.

One or two pieces of rock from the roof hit us as they fell, but we were being beaten to death by sound.

Then suddenly came the most frightful crack of all. The girl shrieked. Gleist blasphemed in screaming German. I kept my teeth tight shut to stop myself yelling too.

The shattering roar split the very darkness. With frightful suddenness, daylight burst into the blackness like a solid attack on the nerves.

As it came, blinding us completely, the awful storm of noise began to run away into the distance, like some shouting giant speeding off far away.

I think we all had our eyes shut against the glare. All I could see was brilliant patches of colour in my retina. When I opened my eyes they stayed floating before my sight.

The sound went. The noise of rushing water from somewhere just did not register for a minute or more, we were so deafened by the onslaught.

'The cave — split!' Gleist said, his voice

grinding. 'Look!'

The roof of the vast place was riven by a gash at least thirty feet across and hundreds of feet long. The crack ran at right-angles to where the beam had run.

I let the girl go and went back to the edge where the beam had been. The drop was nearly two hundred feet and far below there was a stream frothing and jumping along a crooked rocky course.

'That must be new,' I said as the girl joined me. 'We would have heard it before otherwise. Well, at least we can see where we are.'

'And where are we?' she snapped. 'Up a gum tree! We can't get down there or jump that!'

She pointed across the gap where the beam had run. It was forty feet wide and some of the other lip had broken away.

I looked down the cliff beneath our feet. Not being a mountaineer or rock climber I couldn't see any way down it.

'There is a way out there,' Gleist said, wiping his face. 'Look.'

He pointed down to the stream where it ran to the left. There was a great crack in the rock through which it was pouring and the green of trees in the valley could be seen through it.

'But we can't jump down there!' the girl said.

'You could not climb that,' Gleist said, kneeling and peering over the edge. 'It is a sheer break down for thirty metres.'

'We can't stay here and starve,' I said. 'Funnily enough, you can't eat diamonds. This is a Midas situation. I always get mixed up with Midas and the giant in *Jack and the Beanstalk*.'

'This is a hell of a time for fairy tales!' she said furiously.

'Not a fairy tale, science fiction,' I said. 'He grew a mighty beanstalk from a bean mutation. We can make one, a stalk perhaps.'

'I didn't see any rope back there,' she said, as I turned to walk into the tunnel again.

'Nor did I,' I agreed. 'But we can look.'

We all went back and searched amongst the cases and frames but there was no rope. All the cases had been nailed.

'So now what?' she said sulkily and sat on a case.

'Plait one,' I said. 'There's enough straw and packing rags here to make a rope a mile long.'

'Blimey!' she said, staring. 'You wouldn't risk yourself on a thing like that?'

'It's better than starving,' I said, pulling armfuls of straw out of a case. 'Come on. Get as much out as you can and then start sorting the lengths.'

'This is crazy,' Gleist said. 'But it is a chance, perhaps. I do not want to starve. I nearly did once. It is terrible. It is the worse death. We crashed in a desert. Himmel! I am scared of it even now.'

He started to pull straw out of the cases. She just sat there, sulking. I was getting very tired of her mercurial character. It was too unstable.

'Get working,' I said, angrily. 'You get no eat till we've finished.'

'A hundred feet,' she said. 'You can't plait all that!'

'We have to try. That's the object of the exercise. Start sorting. Longest bits over there.'

We started off. It took hours. It was ironic to be surrounded by all the wealth any trio could ever want in this world and to be dependent on a kind of prison job routine for the next sandwich.

I must confess that the more we worked the hungrier I felt. I hadn't eaten since morning, and we'd had a hard time since. I even stopped looking up at the unattainable fish swimming above us. I kept thinking of catching one. I could even taste it.

The others must have felt the same for we stopped talking altogether and just concentrated on weaving that fantastic rope.

It got longer, but it still seemed only a yard or two long. But the more used to the work we got, the faster the rope grew.

'Isn't that enough?' she said. 'My fingers are going to wear through.'

I paced it out. Twenty-one. We were getting on.

'Half as much again,' I said.

'Oh Christ!' she moaned.

'Make the rope!' Gleist shouted as if commanding an army troop.

She looked at him in surprise and then went on working. It was the first time I had known her not to answer back.

We went on, fumbling with weary hands. Our fingers hurt, our wrists ached. I began to think of this whole expedition as one torment after another. Never in my life had such a run of bad luck hit me as did that excursion after a friend's daughter. She was a jinx.

'I want a drink,' she said huskily.

'The water's down there at the end of the rope when it's finished,' I said.

'No!' she said, jumping up. 'There was some in the other cave. I remember now. In a crack in the wall somewhere.'

She went into the far cave. We went on working. He started to mumble some marching song, but it would have been a damn slow march.

It began to get on my nerves and I kept biting back telling him to shut up. She came back, wiping her face with a handkerchief. She had washed the dirt and smudges off and looked pretty.

She put the handkerchief back into her pocket and felt the diamonds there, because she looked quickly at Gleist as he bent over the rope making.

'It must be long enough now,' she said, sitting on her box.

'Get on with it and do not talk!' Gleist commanded, and then went on mumbling his tune with a belligerent air.

She got on with her next bit. We were making lengths as long as we could and then tying them together. Testing it, the rope seemed quite strong enough. It depended on the knots all being sound.

We plodded on. Twice more I paced it and then it seemed long enough. We went back through the tunnel to the ledge. Evening sun was streaming in golden bars through the great rent in the roof.

I took the rope and let it over the ledge, hand over hand. It wasn't long enough. We had to reach the beginning of the more broken rock below which we could easily climb down over. But we couldn't drop and land on it without a certain broken leg.

So back we went. Gleist cursed and sang louder, as if he were beating somebody to the time. We sat down and made more links. It wasn't easy to judge how many more were wanted, looking down on the rope from above, but I reckoned ten. So we made ten and went back to the ledge.

This time it got to within a safe distance of the broken rocks below.

The next problem was how to fix the upper end.

There were pit props lying in the tunnel, beams whose wedges had fallen out. After a search I found one that spanned the mouth of the tunnel horizontally. There were a lot of the old wooden wedges lying around and not all rotten.

With a few of these and the butt of the rifle, we wedged the beam tightly across the opening. Then we shoved against it and sat hard on it and made sure it would hold. It did.

We lashed the end of the straw rope round it, and let the rest drag down to the broken rocks below.

'Okay,' I said. 'I'd better go first. It was my brain-child. I ought to risk it.'

They didn't argue. The girl kept looking at the jammed beam, wondering if it would stay there.

I went over the edge and started to climb down. The straw was slippery. I had to go knot by knot to get a grip at all. It creaked and stretched alarmingly and once I thought it would part altogether.

I stopped there, listening to the creaking straw. Above me I could see their white, staring faces watching me.

'Is it all right?' she shouted.

'So far,' I said.

I went on down. The rope started to swing then, for the wall was further in than the ledge and I could not reach it to steady myself.

Then it started to spin. I went round and round with sickening slowness. With the weakness of hunger and sheer tiredness I began to feel sick and dizzy.

'Are you all right?' I heard her scream out above.

That was when I started to let go.

★　★　★

I slid as my grasp weakened. The knots, passing upwards tried to smash my hands away altogether. The pain of that cleared

160

my head partially and I grabbed hard to stop the downfall. The last knot almost broke my fingers. I heard the girl scream as I closed my eyes to stop the dizziness.

When I opened them again I was hanging, still slowly turning, but within foot reach of the wall again. I put a foot out and steadied the movement until it died.

I felt better then and went on down until I could touch the broken rock with my feet. I got a stand and kept upright as I looked up the rope to the ledge. It seemed a hundred miles high.

'Okay!' I shouted. 'Now look. Watch that spin in the middle. You can't touch the wall. Try and get down that bit fast or you'll start dizziness. Get me?'

'All right!' the girl said. 'I'm coming next.'

As her legs and bottom came over the edge I shouted again.

'Don't forget the middle bit!'

I watched her coming down with painful slowness. Sometimes she seemed to stop altogether and I held my breath, but she came on again. I held the end of the rope in the hope it would steady the spin tendency.

No luck. The creaking rope began to turn as she came to no man's land in the middle. I saw her stop climbing and just hang there. My heart jumped.

'Come down quick!' I shouted. 'Don't hang there! Keep climbing!'

She was going round and round, just clinging there like a human spider at the start of a web.

'Keep going, for God's sake!'

She stayed there, spinning, caught by the same trick as I had been.

But then she started to move again. Slowly, fumbling, her feet slipping on the rope. She was dizzy.

Any moment I thought she would lose it and fall, but she clung on, stopping, starting down again, stopping . . .

At last she reached the nearest part of the wall again. I saw her boots kicking to get hold of it and stop the slow spin. She did it and stayed there a long time, resting, clearing her head.

After a while she came on down. As she came beside me she let go the rope and just fell against me, clinging to me to keep her upright.

We almost fell together over the rocky slope, but I managed to keep a footing and we just didn't.

'Blimey, what a ride!' she gasped, and started to laugh breathlessly.

I looked up. Gleist was looking down over the edge. He did not seem in a hurry to come down.

'Watch the middle span!' I shouted.

He did not answer but just stared down at us.

I had let go the rope which was swinging aimlessly, creaking and swishing.

'What's the matter?' I called up.

The girl had got over the giggles and looked up as well.

'What's he up to?' she said.

Until she said that I had had no suspicion of Gleist in the position he was in. My only view had been that having watched us swinging almost to death he was scared to try the climb down himself.

Her tricky female mind saw it differently, and it came as a shock.

His face disappeared. He had gone

back from the ledge.

Then I remembered the rifle.

That weapon was too big, too awkward to be carried down a climb like that one. I had left it up there deliberately, as anyway, I still had the revolver which my companion had handed over at the outset.

'Gleist!' I shouted up and my voice echoed.

He didn't show, didn't answer. I looked around. We stood on broken rock and the way down was steep and very broken, not the sort of country to allow fast travel.

And no cover.

'What's he up to?' she said again.

'Something bad,' I said. 'Start going down. Look for a big rock to get under. I don't care for this.'

If he shot us where we stood, and a hundred feet was nothing to a rifle, then his way was clear of us. He would have no need to fear our talking about the treasure once we were out in the world again.

We never would get out in the world again.

164

We started down the rocky slope, slipping and sliding a lot so that loose stones rattled away. I tried to keep my eyes turned up to the ledge as much as I could, but on that ground one had to watch carefully where one trod or break an ankle.

His face showed. A moment later I saw the barrel of the rifle under it as he started to squint in taking aim.

'Keep moving. It's coming,' I said.

I heard her gasp. I got the revolver out of my pocket and took a quick potshot. The head ducked back. He hadn't expected it. My shot hit the ledge and ricocheted with a jazzy scream.

'The war's on!' I said. 'Don't stop till you see a shelter!'

She trod the broken rock so lightly, leaping from one to another that it seemed like a dance.

The face appeared again, and this time the rifle fired. I dodged backwards, assuming he was firing a bit ahead to cover my movement.

The shot hit a rock ahead of me and screamed off. I fired back twice. One hit the ledge, the other must have nearly hit him for he ducked back out of sight again.

I am a rarity in that I am a revolver shot in constant practice. Even so, a hundred feet upwards from a bad base were bad conditions. Added to that the light, split by the solid yellow beams of the evening sun, was distracting from any sort of true aim.

He was on an easier street. He had an accurate weapon, and the light was behind him.

This time I didn't go on, but kept watching the ledge until I saw the edge of his head appear again. I let it come on till his eyes showed, then I fired.

I missed him, but drove him back. Also I guessed he would wait a bit before showing his head again, unless he heard me moving.

The going was loose and the rocks rocked under me as I went on down, almost falling from one to the other in the steep decline.

Another shot came, but this time it tore my shirt sleeve and I just spun off any old how and landed on my knees between two big rocks.

I plugged up another bullet as a second shot came. I don't know what happened to either round, but his head went back again.

He had fired at me because the girl was not in sight any more. I scrambled out over the rocks and down again.

My head kept twisting up but he didn't show. For a brief time I got the old hopeful uprush in me that I'd hit him.

'Here!'

Her voice cried out as I slithered over a big wet rock and another shot cracked against it. The bullet ripped off, screamed, must have turned in the air for it fell, battered on my back.

I thought I'd been shot by a live round, but rolled in under the big boulder where she was sheltering.

'Nasty man,' she said.

This was a brief respite, for the stream was still fifty feet below, and I could see no cover on the way down at all. I gave her the gun.

'Recharge,' I said. 'We need all we can stuff into it.'

She filled the fired chambers and gave the gun back to me. I crouched there, peering upwards round the edge of the boulder.

Gleist showed head and shoulders now, trying to see where we had gone. He had a narrow field to search for he had almost hit me a half-minute before and knew I could not have gone far, but he couldn't trace us.

He had the rifle ready, but it would take him a second to take proper aim. A quickfire would be a wild one, with the odds against it reaching a target.

Working on that gamble I showed my head and took aim at him. I fired. He went back. I knew I'd got his shoulder then. I'd seen his instant reaction to the hurt.

'I think I got him,' I said. 'A wing shot.'

'Let's get down there then!' she said.

'Better wait and see. He'll be cross now, even if he's not badly torn.'

We waited. I kept watch on the ledge for three or four minutes, but he didn't show. I began to hope, but remembered it could be an old trick of the sniper to fake hurt.

'Let's go,' she said.

'No.'

'But he must be — '

'I've got a feeling.'

She started up. I grabbed her shoulder and pulled her back again. She tried to shake my hand off and it hurt her when I grabbed harder.

She was showing from above where she stood, struggling. I made a big effort and heaved her back into cover.

'He's not there!' she panted. 'Let me go!'

I held her dead tight then by letting go her shoulder and getting my arm right round her tummy as she tried to twist away. I clamped her tight to me and stood her kicking as I looked upwards again.

'Quiet, you little idiot! He's up there.'

She stopped dead in my arm. We both stared up at the ledge. There was no face showing there, but the rifle was.

It slanted upwards towards the broken roof of the vast cave. As we watched it seemed to waver, or wobble as if the holder was not sure of his aim.

'What's he doing?' she whispered.

'You guess,' I said. 'I'm tired.'

Nothing happened. The rifle went on wavering there and then was drawn down out of sight.

When the anger at this turnabout situation had subsided somewhat, the mystery of his behaviour became clearer.

He could not have been sure of getting both of us by his shooting, even with a rifle, for from above it was impossible to tell what rocks gave cover down where we were.

Yet he had risked either shooting us maybe not even dead, or of letting us hide. That meant he could never have come down that rope until he had killed us.

It seemed lunatic, when I came to think of it.

He fired at the roof. It made a hell of a row, echoing the shot and screaming of the ricochet a dozen times.

'Why did he do that?' she whispered.

'Don't ask me.'

We watched. The rifle barrel had gone back out of sight.

'He must be hit,' she said. She still

talked as if somebody might be right behind, eavesdropping.

'I know he is, but how badly? That's the point.'

'Let's risk it. I'm getting the creeps.'

'Its creepier with a bullet in your back.'

'He can't shoot any more or he wouldn't have done that.'

'If we had a hat we could try that old trick again. I don't want to try it with you. Think a moment. Whatever he's doing up there, if he can still fire he must shoot us now. He can't shake hands after this lot.'

'But if he can't shoot? You hit his shoulder — '

'I think I hit his shoulder. He fired at the roof. Perhaps he tried to fire through that crack or fired to make as much noise as possible. He said he had friends who were with him somewhere.'

'I'd forgotten them. But do you believe that?'

'It's safer to, isn't it?'

She looked away down the rocky slope to the roaring torrent of the stream. It gushed out through the crack and into the valley as if mad to go.

'They could get in there,' she said.

'But that way has only just been broken through,' I said. 'They're not likely to know of it so soon. It happened under our noses. It'd be a different matter looking for it from the outside.'

'They could see the water.'

'If they were out there looking, but Gleist came in the normal route. He knew where the treasure was. Why would his mates look outside?'

I was still watching the ledge. He was moving up there. The slanting beam of sunlight was catching something that reflected up the rock wall above him.

It could have been the rifle, or some part of it. Whatever it was moved right along from the end of the ledge back to the tunnel mouth.

She saw it, too.

'What's he doing?'

'Crawling about. A restless person. He might get a better angle shot at us from back there.'

She didn't say any more. Just watched the light spot on the rock wall. It stopped again.

She tricked me then. She twisted, jumped, sprang off one foot up on to a rock and then started down the incline stumbling, slipping and almost falling but keeping on.

I looked back up at the ledge. His head appeared at the end near the tunnel and then I saw the rifle trained on her as she ran stumblingly down the slope. He had to steady his aim, her progress was too wild for him to take a crack shot.

He did not see me, or did not care. I fired. Nothing happened. He fired and she stumbled a last time and disappeared with a yell somewhere down the slope.

8

I didn't see where she fell, only that she did. I thought Gleist had hit her for when I twisted my neck and looked up at him again he was standing there near the edge, the rifle dropped in his hands as if he had no further use for it.

But I saw something was wrong as I raised my pistol to fire again.

He dropped the rifle. His arms went flaccid at his sides. He stood there looking at the cracked roof, and then he began to sink.

He staggered forward, as if to keep his balance against his fall, but he couldn't. He pitched headfirst over the edge and came whirling down, a dummy with loose arms and legs, from the overhang.

The tumbled masses of the rock above me prevented me seeing his death crash. Thank heaven for that. I drew what comfort I could from thinking that perhaps he was dead before he broke up on the rocks.

I got up then and began to scramble down the slope, slipping and sliding, loosening small stones that raced away from me and rattled down to the water.

As I went I searched behind the larger rocks, but found nothing of her at all. I shouted and my voice echoed in the great cavern. The rushing of the stream was the only other sound.

I felt then she had certainly been hit. That she didn't answer because she couldn't. My tensions, relieved for a little by the death of the rifleman, returned again at the thought that he had got her first.

The rocks were scattered, tumbled and fallen in such a mass that there were a thousand places where she might have fallen and could not now be seen.

My search was almost hopeless from the start but I kept on desperately hoping to see some sign of her. I found none.

The only way was to try and make some systematic sweep of the slope, scrambling along in parallel lines with the stream, starting about the spot where I had last seen her.

I went on until I began to feel the soles had been torn off my shoes and I was treading the sharp, broken stone with bare feet. I sat down to rest, hot and weary.

The daylight through the crack was growing less now as the sun died away over the mountains. Soon I would not be able to search any more, so I got up and started on again.

The first I saw of them was a shadow on the rock before me, just caught by the sun's last rays. When I turned, the first solid object of theirs I saw was the muzzle of a Mauser pointing dead between my eyes.

'Achtung!' the man said, quite unnecessarily.

I straightened up slowly, thankful that my gun was in my pocket. Otherwise I would have been shot before any danger of my shooting developed.

'Where is Gleist?' the man said.

He was a tall, dark fellow in shirt and shorts, stockings and heavy shoes, Tyrolean without decorations. There were two more men down by the stream, standing looking up.

'Gleist fell off the ledge up there,' I said and pointed.

He pushed the gun forward sharply.

'Don't worry. I know the rules,' I said, shrugging. 'Never fight a Mauser with bare fists.'

He grinned briefly and glanced up at the ledge, also briefly.

'We got stranded up there,' I said. 'The bridge fell down with the earthquake or whatever it was. We made the rope. When I got down he fired at me with a rifle. I think he got over-excited and fell off.'

'If he is dead, good,' the man said. 'He was going forward on his own. That is the doublecross. He knew the way. We did not.'

'So he ditched you?' I said, easing up a bit.

'That is the word, I think.'

'And you still don't know the way?'

He looked quickly round but the gun was kept steady on me.

'It must be near here,' he said. 'Perhaps you know, also?'

'The way where? I'm looking for the way out of here. I was making for that crack before the daylight goes.'

I pointed down to where the stream was gushing and frothing out into the gathering twilight.

'You were up there with Gleist,' he said. 'Did he tell you why he was there?'

'There is a weird collection of Tatty up there,' I said. 'Some lunatic must have done it. I never saw such a load of muck.'

The man looked strange at that. He frowned and cocked his head, watching me.

'Is that all?'

'All? There's about fifteen tons of it. Sort of thing they wouldn't give as prizes at a shooting gallery. I never saw anything like it.'

'I can hardly believe you.'

'Go and see. If you're a patriot you might agree the sentiment, but the art — Himmel, as you say. It's atrocious.'

He watched me still, considering whether I was lying but I think he decided I wouldn't dare with a Mauser at my head and two of his friends within call, probably also equipped with suitable aggressive ironwork.

'Up there?' he said.

'Down that tunnel. You can just see the opening.'

'Gleist would not have risked double-crossing us for the sake of rubbish,' he said.

'Did he know what it was? We didn't till we saw it. He seemed surprised.' I had nearly let out the girl's existence with that 'we' and made up quickly to shove Gleist in.

At this time my tension over her was acute. I certainly didn't want her to be found by these gentlemen if she was hurt or if she wasn't, but even just hiding from them.

I just wouldn't look at the possibility that she might be dead. I do now that I know she wasn't, but at that time it made me go sick and cold, and I don't like that.

I didn't like any part of the situation. Tired mentally and exhausted physically, the suspense of not getting out of this place was going on too long.

There was this man with the gun, but at that point I really didn't care much if he fired it or not.

'There must be something more,' he said keenly. 'Something perhaps you did not see. It was promised for The Movement. Nobody would dare fool such a body. There must be something more than what you say.'

'Go up and look,' I said. 'We made a rope. It takes the weight.'

He stared at our knotted straw creation doubtfully, as it twisted slowly and untwisted again.

At least I had learned something. That treasure had been hidden probably with the idea of financing The Movement when it finally became possible. A resurrection of the Nazi cult with a few millions in the kitty to begin with.

I was surprised I hadn't thought of that before. All along I had thought it some mad, greedy dream of a drunken, defeated general scurrying to what he thought might be future security.

I hadn't thought of something much bigger.

If it was The Movement I was up against, then it would be fair to think that

I stood little chance, if any, of getting out of this hellhole.

The doublecrosser had not been Gleist the son alone, but von Gleist the father, shot in the back by Ferdi, perhaps deservingly as I saw it now. For without any doubt at all, von G., feeling at the end of his tether had tried to raise money from Ferdi and at the same time had tipped off The Movement.

So that his intention had been to sell something he had already given away to a powerful body of men who could be relied on to wipe out Ferdi and his feeble lieutenants.

Like father, like son, young Gleist had tried to ditch his companions, The Movement, the girl and me, roughly that order. Then I realised I had forgotten Ferdi.

Ferdi was probably in the deepest ditch of all, for sooner or later he would meet the force of The Movement, specially when they knew he had shot one of their aged generals in the back.

The man turned and looked down at his henchmen.

'Hans. Martin. Come up.'

The two men started to clamber up the rocky slope. I watched tensely in case they saw her lying there somewhere, but they came on up, a couple of Teutonic blonds, dour, hard-eyed die-for-the-Movement boys.

One had a scar like an old burn on his jaw. This one the leader called Martin.

'Get up the rope,' the leader said in German. 'See if anything is up there.'

Martin went. He had one hell of a job because of the rope spinning, but he made it at last. I was sitting on the rock then, smoking a cigarette. The leader did not mind my digging in my pockets for cigarettes and lighter. He was so confident of his mastery of the situation that he did not fear any tricks from me.

That attitude dispelled some of my tiredness, and I began to think that there might be a way round these representatives of The Movement.

Martin scrambled over the ledge and vanished.

'Why have you come here?' the leader said.

'Sheer ruddy accident. I got mistaken for somebody else and some men chased me here with guns in my back. I had to drive mighty fast and finally drove over a ledge and had to hide the car, then hide myself in these mines.'

The leader watched me.

Hans turned to him.

'The Mercedes hidden under the sacks back by the road, perhaps,' he said in German.

'That's the one,' I said.

They both turned on me quickly.

'You speak German?' the leader snapped.

'No. Mercedes is the same in any language.' I didn't think it wise to say I could. I can a bit, and understand more, but I didn't want to become involved by them thinking I was anti-Movement or anything political.

My opinion was justified, for the leader eased off.

'There is a bullet in the tyre and it has burnt, too,' he said.

'I told you. It was a sharp ride.'

They looked at each other.

'Who fired at you?' Hans asked.

'Some Spaniards. I never got round to finding out why. It took all my time getting away from them.'

'There must be a reason.' Hans was silky, menacing.

'The reason must be they mistook me for somebody else. I'd never seen them before.'

'Very curious,' Hans said. 'There must be some stronger reason, I think. Not just a mistake. Perhaps they saw you with somebody they wanted to talk to.'

'The way they behaved they couldn't have expected to talk with anybody but an undertaker.'

Hans got up from where he had squatted to talk to me.

'I will go find Gleist,' he said, and started clambering up the rocks towards the rope.

I didn't want that. Gleist's body would show he had been shot, probably twice, once in the shoulder and the last one that had — one way or the other — killed him.

In my saying I had been alone, this would prove against me that I had a gun.

Which meant that if I did not use it in the next minute or two, I wouldn't have anything at all.

I smoked on, listening to Hans's boots scrabbling on the rocks. It was louder than the water below and it meant more to me.

My cigarette was short by then. The leader was splitting his sight between watching me and glancing up to see Hans's progress.

Now was the time or there would be no time at all.

Hans was getting near the sheer cliff and Gleist's body was somewhere there. As Martin hadn't seen it, it couldn't be very obvious. It might take a few seconds to find.

The gun was hard in my pocket. But it was in my pocket. Some legendary Westerner might snatch a gun from a well-greased holster in a split second. He would never have got one out of a pocket before he got shot.

The leader watched me. My tiredness shook off. It had to. Timing was essential now, and every movement accurate.

His eyes flickered up to Hans again.

I flicked the cigarette end. It got his right eye and burst into a shower of sparks. As it hit, I dived forward off the rock I sat on and got his leg.

The Mauser fired somewhere above me and the leader yelled.

I didn't blame him.

*   *   *

Hans twisted round on the rock up the slope. I saw him as I brought the leader crashing down beside me and got a hold on his blindly waving wrist. I cracked the gun out of his hold by twisting his wrist till it was going to break.

Several shots came down from Hans, and in another brief glimpse I saw him scrambling back down the rocks towards us.

The leader was half-blind. I got the Mauser and knocked him right out with it. Then I fired a couple of shots up at Hans. He ducked down behind a rock for cover.

Suddenly Martin appeared up on the ledge.

'It's up here!' he shouted down. 'What's the firing?'

I put one up at him. For an instant he didn't seem to get the drift, then he ducked down behind the ledge. I could expect some fire from him in a second or two.

Some came down from Hans, but only one round. He had already fired two. I wondered if he was mean because he had no reserve ammo. That wasn't the sort of guess to bet on. He could have been mean anyway.

The situation was that I was in command of a hole with the leader and myself in it, and with no way out that wasn't covered by Hans and Martin.

It would seem that I had so far got nowhere and might well have spoilt my slim chances of any further existence.

There was no other way for me but to pursue a clumsy and painful course by carrying the leader on my back, as bullet absorbing material, and to try and stumble down to the river with him.

Tired and aching, it wasn't a pleasant proposition, but the other was death.

Martin fired down two rounds which hit rocks and went screaming. They couldn't have hit me. They were a show of force.

I put the Mauser in my other pocket, then got the leader's arms over my shoulders and hoicked him on my back. Then we started clambering over the rocks, slipping and stumbling as if I was a drunk bringing home a worse one.

There was no firing. Hans and Martin respected their leader.

He was a hell of a weight. With the rough going and my tiredness, let alone bruises, it was like an exquisite torture, agony so acute it was almost a pleasure.

We staggered and rolled and almost fell a dozen times.

Then, near the water, I heard stones clattering down behind me. I dropped the leader's right hand, got the Mauser from my pocket and turned in time to see Hans jumping and slithering down the slope behind us.

I fired a shot at him. Not particularly to

hit him, just to bring him up. But you never can tell with a wild shot. It blew his hat off and he dropped like a log on his face.

It must have hurt, that fall, but he did it himself.

The leader still covered half of me. Martin made a wild shot from the ledge. I heard it whistle by.

'Stand back from there!' Martin shouted.

The words re-echoed half a dozen times. I didn't know what he meant. He seemed to me, like Hans, to be shaken very easily, for members of a Movement.

That's what I thought then, because as I stood there, half-shielded by a dead weight of flesh, I could not see Ferdi appear on the opposite side of the cavern, at the tunnel mouth which once had been joined with Martin's ledge.

Martin fired. I saw that he shot, not at me, but right across the cavern. I half-turned then and saw Ferdi.

Five shots sounded in quick succession, and Martin danced back into the tunnel mouth with bits of small stone and dust flying off the walls around him.

I turned my man a little and saw Ferdi on the ledge. He had a big man with him, Digger or Pommie, perhaps. That man had a sub-machine-gun in his formidable grasp.

My burden became lighter at the double usefulness his hulk now gave, for I was sure Ferdi would drill me, too, if he could.

Another typewriter burst of shots rang out. Bullets shrieked away from the rocks round the prostrate Hans.

I began stumbling and swaying down the rocks again. Soon I was sloshing in the edge of the stream. Ferdi shouted some order from up above but the noise of the water was too close now for me to hear what he said.

The crack in the wall was a dozen yards away from me. The edge of the stream bed was uneven, but better than the broken rocks I had trodden so far.

The firing got brisk. The Germans were pushing it out hard now and Ferdi's typewriter seemed to be silenced. But as I reached the crack it rattled out again and for a while I heard no revolver shots in answer.

They started again as I pushed

through, the water up to my thighs, tugging at me furiously. We got through to the other side.

It was a grassy slope with a few bushes and some scrubby looking, scattered trees. I let the leader down to the grass.

Four men saw me do it. They had Lugers. They were dressed like the other Germans. One man detached from the rest, went to the crack and looked in to see what the battle was doing.

I just stood there as the other three came up. It just wasn't worth constantly trying, when round every corner there was a new set of bastards waiting.

'Well done,' the foremost man said in German.

The shock was weakening, but encouraging. They thought I had carried their wounded leader from the fracas inside, had rescued him, in fact.

I shrugged. When the leader came to, that would be the end of the misunderstanding. Best not to wait for that.

'You're wanted in there, I should think,' I said. 'Your two have a machine-gun to cope with.'

'You are English!'

All three of them looked surprised, but a fresh burst of firing from the cave convinced them I was right.

The man on watch at the crack called back to them.

They ran towards the crack. I ran the other way, skirting the bushes and trees until I could no longer see the crack.

Then I got down on my knees, drank water and washed my face. It was ice cold. I never thought I'd get to like plain water. Perhaps it had something from the mountains that made it different.

I got up and went on, bearing round to the right. The blue evening was on then, but it was still very light and clear.

The valley curved round and then ended in a steep gully that ran up three or four hundred feet. Some way up it I saw something white lying on the grass and rock. A cigarette packet.

Then this must be a way out of the mountain prison. Someone had used it. Possibly the Germans.

The difficulty then was that I did not know where the girl was, whether she was hurt or what had happened to her. I had the feeling that if I got up that gully, I would get out and away from this unpleasant business altogether.

But after all this, I couldn't leave the girl. That would be a complete economic waste of time, money, suffering and nervous endurance. That is why I rarely give up. I am bloody minded and always want my money's worth or my own back.

To go up the gully might free me, but the way I was thinking I would have to go back into the mine again, and it was occupied by warring factions, one of which was bound to win. The winner would still be armed.

None of the possible winners was going to believe I had gone back for a reason like trying to find a girl when there were a million or two lying just round the bend.

Furthermore, when the leader came to he would say I'd tried to burn his eye out and had then brained him with a pistol. This would persuade the others that I was not, as appeared, on their side.

But if Ferdi, with his automatic weapons, won? Would that be any better?

Ferdi was within smelling distance of the loot. Therefore his original need for me to join in no longer existed.

It appeared I had no friend in the mountain.

I sat down a moment on a rock and shut my eyes, trying to think back to when the girl had fled for the last time. My attention had been sharply divided by Gleist above me with the rifle.

The girl had fallen or ducked down, thrown herself behind a rock. But she hadn't been there when I looked later. I felt sure of that now.

The remaining possibility then was that she had got out of the crack. But if she had done that she must have been behind the Germans when they came in.

She must have been still in the cavern, for by going out she would have met the Teutonic three. After they had appeared, she must have gone out through the crack.

But I had been looking to the Germans whose backs were to the water, and I should have seen her —

The water! Damn it!

She could have hidden in the stream which was no more than two feet deep and most of that froth. She could have hidden there and then wormed her way down in the water without anybody seeing.

To me then it seemed the only possible explanation.

Once again she had left me to my fate and done a bolt. Could the reason be the same as before?

She had been hard to tear away from the loot. Had she gone back with some hare-brained idea of collecting a lot more than she had got already in her bulging pockets?

If so. How?

Then I remembered the treasure cave and the queer circular windows where the fish circled and twisted.

The lake.

I added up roughly the height of the treasure cave above the valley I was in and made it about three hundred feet. No climb at all if you could find a way up.

Add a bit more for the depth of the water, then the height of the banks of the lake and it still didn't sound formidable.

I went back, using the trees and bushes for cover from anyone near the crack in the rock. From there I heard desultory shots. The battle was still on. While it still flourished it was unlikely that anyone would be out looking for me.

I got round the danger point. The valley opened out, its sides becoming less sheer, great slopes of patchy grass and scrub. I turned up the left-hand slope. It was still hard going but manageable.

At the top the ground levelled out and there was a clump of trees not far off. Beyond that the side of the mountain rose up in terrifying grandeur.

Its side was scarred and fresh gashes showed where rocks had broken away and rolled down. It was from this monster that the avalanches had rained down on the mine.

Even then, close to the trees there was a monstrous pile of stones heaped up, but tilting, as if about to topple over. I went on towards the trees. Trees seemed to indicate water. Perhaps I was thinking of oases, but it turned out to be right in this case.

When I came to the trees the ground sloped away, grassy but broken with grey rocks, to a lake about a hundred yards across.

On the left the terrible pile of huge stones stood, its reflection clear in the water as if it had begun to fall already.

There were signs that the lake had been artificially cut, for the sides were fairly regular, and at the far end there was a sluice gate. It had been constructed to provide water power for some part of the mine.

This changed the outlook and I took a good look round.

If there had been a water-wheel and the lake had been cut out and earth carted out, then there must have been some kind of road up here. Which meant an old way down on the far side of the mountain from the road we'd been chased on.

This was encouraging. The girl still had the map. As a map it was useless unless you knew where you were to start with. But if you knew, then its use began to be more apparent.

She had chosen the tunnel approach

because then it had been the better of perhaps two ways. But when the bridge had fallen, this upper way must have been the alternative and presumably much more dangerous.

A moon was coming up in the purple sky. It started to shimmer its edge on the water and the mountain was etched with silver so that it stood out against the blue background.

It was very clear, very still. I saw nothing moving but a fish who jumped and the ripples spreading from him made the moon rock in the water.

The only works showing were the distant sluice gate, and I started to walk round the ridge towards it. The growing moonlight made the trees look alive, like people standing, watching. Several times I thought I saw someone moving in their shadows.

The truth was I had got too damn tired to be really sure of what I was seeing. But there was a consolation in that the girl would be tired too. Tired people are careless. I hoped she would be.

Near to the old baulks of timber

forming the water gate I saw something move over by the rusted gear wheels and chains. I got into the shadow of a tree and watched.

To the right the ground sloped away sharply into a ravine. It was fairly shallow. The waterway ran down in a steep channel to the bottom where some of the old mine workings could be seen, white as ghosts in the moonlight.

I made out the shadow more clearly, and heard the clank of chains. I could not see for sure but I felt it must be the girl.

She was trying to free the mechanism.

She was going to let the water out of the lake. It was a lot of water. If it got down into those workings below it would flood the whole of this part of the mine. It would end the battle down there.

It would end all the men as well.

9

The simplicity of her scheme to outdo all enemies was shocking. Given the strength to release the rusty mechanism, she had to win. All the fighting men down in the tunnels would be washed away, drowned. The water would go down and down with them, leaving the treasure caves dripping, but safe.

Her shadow in the moonlight looked desperately determined in its attitudes. She was so completely intent on releasing the great cogs that she didn't see me come up on her.

'Hallo,' I said.

She started back with a little cry, and it took her a moment to recover.

'Why don't you give this loot up?' I said. 'We can get away now. This grassy stretch winding away was a road and goes somewhere. Best thing we can do is find out where.'

She wiped the palms of her hands on

her thighs and smiled. She didn't answer.

'Shall I carry you?' I said. 'Or put a halter on you and lead you down? One of the two. I've had just enough of your frisky bolts. This time we're going home!'

'You sound too damn serious,' she said.

'I am damn serious.'

The chains and cogs behind her grunted. It was a startling sound in the still night.

'Did you free those gears?' I said. 'Stand aside!'

She bent and picked up something from the patchy grass at her feet. She showed it to me a brief instant. It was a piece of iron with a ring on the end.

The locking pin to the machinery. She laughed and tossed it out into the water.

The machinery was holding by rust alone, hence the grunting as the weight of the water pressed against the water gates.

'You're a bright little crook!' I shouted at her.

I started to hunt round the stones and grass the machinery stood on in case there was something, a piece of broken steel or chain — anything that would jam the gears tight and stop the gates opening.

As I searched, the machine grunted again. From the waterway I heard a growing hissing of water sluicing down the channel to the mine works below.

'Leave it!' she shouted. 'Why do you care? They tried to kill us! Let them drown!'

'Charming. Why don't you join a witch club?'

I tried to get a bolt out that was loose in a hole in the frame. It had almost rusted through. I hit it with the butt of the Mauser and it broke.

But the holes the original locking pin had gone through had moved apart through the slow, grunting movement of the gears. I shoved the bolt between the teeth and hoped that might do it.

Bits of it crumbled into rust flakes, but it jammed the teeth a bit.

'Get on down the track,' I said, shoving her. 'And don't try any more of your skipping or I'll shoot the boots off your feet. Get on!'

'You're a fool!' she cried. 'There's a

whole fortune down there. We'd be rich for life. Rich, rich as mad! You — '

'You've got a pocketful. Be content and get on!'

I was by then pretty well exhausted in strength and temper and pushed her again. She resisted. I felt like beating her. As I look back on the exasperation of that time I think I damn nearly did.

She went on suddenly to a small clump of trees, then stopped again. Behind us the gears groaned, trying to crush the jamming bolt. I thought, by the sound of it, that they would, eventually. The bolt was too far gone with rust to resist indefinitely.

I stopped with her and looked back at the machine, a black outline in the moonlight. We couldn't see it moving, but the hissing of the water down the chute seemed more intense.

And then we heard something else, a frighteningly familiar sound.

'There's something coming,' she said, and at last she looked really scared.

'That bloody truck!' I said. 'They've found the way!'

'I thought you said they came into the cavern down there?'

'I saw only Ferdi and another man. That leaves two that we know of.'

'Can you see it?'

'I don't even know where this old road ran to. Round the mountain perhaps. Quite likely back to the village.'

The grassy road ran over the lip of the lake wall and by moonlight it wasn't possible to make out where the track ran as the ground beyond was fairly level and a half-mile wide with rising ground on either side.

The sound of the whining truck was echoing in the valley but we saw nothing of it.

'Where is it?' she hissed.

'Sounds nearer than it should be,' I said.

The obvious answer occurred suddenly. That it was actually under the lip of the lake wall coming up to us unseen.

A minute later it proved right. The lumbering vehicle appeared slowly on the rising track, like some hoary giant rising up out of the ocean.

The moon shone on the windscreen, silvering it out so we couldn't see how many men were in it. It rumbled on along the grass track very slowly, in crawler gear.

'Why have they come up here?' she hissed in my ear

'They found another way, as we did. What else?'

'That means the battle's over.'

'And the Movement has lost? I don't know. I shouldn't think that truck could have made the trip round from the road to here in the time. In fact, I'd say, now.'

We crouched under the trees as the big truck went slowly by. Only one man sat in the cab, leaning over the left side, his left elbow sticking out of the window.

He was smoking a cigarette despite his load of explosives so I guessed this must be Pommie.

The truck rumbled to a stop by the machinery. The engine was switched off. Nothing happened.

'What's he doing?' she whispered.

'Waiting, perhaps.'

'What — for the others?' She sounded panicky.

Before I could answer, the cab door opened and Pommie swung down to the ground. He stood a moment, listening, and then he went forward to the machine.

Even from the trees we could hear the jamming bolt crunching as the gears began to crush it. The hissing of the water seemed harder, angrier.

Pommie stood looking at the machinery, then he lifted his head and looked all round him. I could see that he knew somebody was there.

He went back to the truck and leaned against it, looking towards us and the trees. Then he started to come forward along the side of the lorry.

The girl grabbed my arm and held it tightly. I took a pistol from my right-hand pocket. Obviously he could not see us, but the nearer he came the better his chances became.

He stopped just past the tail of the lorry, took the cigarette out of his mouth and flicked it out across the water.

The crunching bolt suddenly groaned

sharply behind him. He whirled round, his fists bunched, ready at his sides. Then he walked back to the machinery and stopped again.

She jogged my arm.

'Get him!' she said. 'Shoot him now!'

'Shut up.' I was glad she didn't have a gun any more. In her present mood of greedy desperation she would have shot everybody within sight.

Pommie stood there by the machinery, head cocked, suspicious but with his back to us. It was as if he could hear something that we could not.

He moved forward, slowly, going past the end of the machine and stopped again, listening.

We could hear the restless crunching of the gear teeth and the steady, menacing hiss of the water in the chute, but nothing else.

He went on, very slowly, very carefully, near to the edge of the ground where it suddenly sloped away down to the working floor below. There he stopped, crouching, looking down at something amongst the old huts down on the working floor.

'What's he doing?' she whispered. 'Why don't you shoot?'

'I think he's waiting for a signal.' I ignored the second question.

'That means the others must be all right,' she said.

Once again I told her to shut up, so that I could listen. Pommie was hearing something, but still I caught nothing of it.

For a moment I thought I heard a whistle — not a man's whistle, but a signal whistle — but it was hard to tell for the water hissing was around the same sort of frequency pitch. It could have been a trick of the water sound.

Watching Pommie I had the feeling he wasn't too sure either.

'Are they his friends?' she said.

'It looks as if it's a surprise, whatever it is, so it isn't likely to be his mates. If it is, then he doesn't trust them, which might help.'

'Anyone would think they wouldn't blow your bloody head off if they caught you again!'

'Keep yours for the time being and be quiet.'

Pommie was moving now, creeping one way, then another, as if to get different views of what he was seeing.

Every time the breaking bolt grunted he looked back at the machinery as if weighing its possibilities. He had the same idea that the girl had actually put into operation, and with which she would have drowned everyone by then but for rust gripping a little too hard.

The truck was quite a few yards from us and with Pommie in a highly suspicious and watchful mood it didn't seem likely that we could reach it without being spotted.

Being spotted meant having to shoot. Shooting meant being heard by whoever was down on the working floor, and there could be a lot of them.

But there was a possible way. I thought that if Pommie had a gun he would have had it out by now, whereas all he had done was to swing his fists as if they were the only weapons.

'We want that truck,' I whispered to her. 'You creep out across to it. Make sure he sees you, but pretend you don't see him. I'll do the rest.'

I should have seen then that the biggest risk wasn't Pommie but the girl. Her greedy little mind was still on the treasure. Or perhaps I was too harsh. Perhaps she just wouldn't give up, no matter what happened.

'All right. But you keep close.'

'Go on. And go slowly.'

She went out, bending, walking almost on tiptoe. It was a good imitation of an imitation of a caricature of a stage effort.

I saw Pommie look round and see her. Obviously he, too, was startled by her attitudes, but he recovered quickly and began to move round to get in behind her. It meant him taking a big, slow curve which brought him closer to the trees than he had been so far.

The thing I was tense about then was that her exaggerated performance would make him think the whole thing was what it was, a put-up job. But he kept on his stalking as if he accepted the apparent situation.

I moved out behind him. The whole thing seemed to be working admirably. I closed up on him from behind.

Then suddenly it happened.

'Okay! Stand still you three! Quite still!'

An automatic rifle of the same kind as Ferdi had had poked over the truck tailboard at us, gleaming in the moonlight like a slice of blue ice. I couldn't see who was in under the canvas top, just the rifle barrel and two hands holding it.

We all stopped obediently. I heard Pommie curse in a muttering sort of way. Obviously he was taken by surprise as much as we were by the sudden appearance of the unwanted.

'Had a ruddy stowaway!' I heard him mutter.

The girl looked back quickly at me, then ahead again.

'Turn your backs,' the gunman said.

The other two did. I didn't move but just stood there.

'Back, soldier. I said turn the back.'

I stood quite still.

'I never turn my back on a gun,' I said. 'It's a superstition.'

The fact was I was then so close to Pommie the marksman couldn't have hit me. Pommie would have absorbed the bullet. Pommie had no such protection for he was quite a yard or two away from the girl.

'Funny man,' the rifleman said.

'Hardly funny. You can see my point.'

I wanted him to talk more before I thought I recognised his voice as being that of the man who had been in the car with Ferdi and I wasn't sure.

If it was, then this was some kind of a double-doublecross. Ferdi hardly knew what he had started on himself.

'I thought you were loyal to Ferdi,' I said. 'This is a surprise.'

Pommie must have recognised the voice, too, when I said that for he let out a volley of vituperation.

'You scrammy little bastard, Louis!' he shouted and half-turned.

'Keep still!' Louis shouted.

'Yes, do that,' I said. 'It helps me.'

Pommie turned back then, still muttering.

The crucial moment now arrived. Louis decided to swing a leg over the tailboard in order to drop to the ground.

In such a manoeuvre a man cannot aim a gun.

As he came over to drop down, the gun in his left hand only, I got the Mauser from my pocket, took a quick bead on him and hit the gun smack in the bullet drum.

He yelled and half-turned to let it go. I got another shot on the stock. That Mauser was accurate and the moonlight was sharp and clear.

The girl ran forward, threw herself headlong and got Louis's leg. She brought him down. He let the gun go and started in on her, kicking and hitting out like mad.

I ran past Pommie but my rescue was not needed. She got Louis one devastating blow somewhere that left him rolling over and over on the grass. He finished up on his face, just panting, trying to make the pain go. She got up. Pommie came cautiously by, watching my Mauser.

'How did you get up here?' I said.

'Ferdi gave me the wire. Something he said. About a water-wheel that had to be high up for driving the stampers down there.' He pointed past the gates machinery. 'Used to take the ore out down there, stamp it, wash it, then take the metal up here by water power, load it and move it off by road. I knew there had to be a pond on top somewhere.'

'You sound like a miner.'

'I was digging copper down Africa way. Shot a nigger. Changed my life, that did. Had to look for something good, then. Something like this.'

'You can't use it by yourself.'

'I don't mean to. I'm with Ferdi. He knows the way out to the market. All I want to do is locate it. Possession is a handy bargainer.'

'It's under the lake,' I said.

He looked up sharply at me. He had watched Louis clambering to his knees, hauling himself up by the truck wheel.

'Under the lake?' he said. 'You sure?'

'We've been there.'

'So that's why they're down there!' Pommie said.

'Who did you see down on the working floor?'

'Some geezers creeping about. Going in

214

the old huts and stamp houses. It's somebody else. There's only four of us, including me and the chizzer.' He pointed to Louis. 'So there couldn't be four of us down there, could there?'

So the Movement had got down there, which must have meant they had located the treasure and were exploring ways of getting it out effectively.

Or did they intend to do it right away?

'Have you seen any other truck around tonight?' I said.

'There's no other trucks about,' he said. 'Just Ferdi's motor. I shoved that out of the road with my front end and went on by.'

'Where?'

'Up to the village.'

'And you found this way from there?'

'It was all grown over. But when you build a village for a mining set-up, you got to have a track from the camp to the mine. That's for sure.'

He looked at Louis leaning against the truck side.

'He must have jumped aboard when I thumped that car out of the road,'

Pommie went on. 'Funny. I didn't see anybody.'

'I thought you were running,' Louis gasped out, holding his stomach region with one hand.

She must have got him with a knee in his wind. It had been very effective.

'You didn't mean to doublecross?' I said curiously.

'What's the good? Ferdi controls the outlet. If you don't have that, you lose out. You can't operate on your own.'

'So that's the only way Ferdi can hold you together?' I said.

'It's good. Strong,' said Louis.

'Suppose Ferdi dies. What then?' I said.

'You mean killed?' said Pommie. 'Who's killing the only man who can turn the stuff into cash?'

'There are other men after it,' I said. 'You saw them down there.'

'Yeah, I know that. But Ferdi's down there, too, isn't he? And Digger? And a machine-gun. They can take care of anything. If Ferdi let that lot come through, there's a reason. He's a tricky little guy.'

The machinery crunked suddenly. All four heads turned towards the cogs, but they were still again. The hissing of the escaping water was steady and seemed unchanged.

'What's wrong with that thing?' Louis said. 'Are the gates giving way?'

'Suppose he is dead?' I persisted. 'What would you do then?'

Louis stared at me.

'We should have to find someone, but Ferdi always makes sure we don't meet anyone who knows. So it would be a start from scratch.'

I was master of this situation because I had two guns. But it is always a bad way to be master. What struck me then was that these two men might be a great help in getting us all out of this place again.

'Ferdi offered me a job in this outfit,' I said.

Louis narrowed his eyes.

'He did? Why?'

'I think he knew there was somebody else after the loot, so he thought more men would be useful.'

'That's true, anyhow,' Pommie said.

217

He went back to the edge where he could see down.

'Are they still down there?' I said.

'They seem to be having a confab,' he said.

'My guess is they can't get the stuff away without a vehicle, so they're waiting for one to come,' I said. 'That means more men on their side.'

Louis hissed out breath.

'Why bother?' the girl said. 'You can drown that lot down there. That would make things easier.'

Louis looked towards the winch. He wasn't as bloodthirsty as my companion.

'Now that we have located what we came for,' he said, 'why add murder? Murder follows you. You do not know when it will come up and tap you on the shoulder. Now that we know the location, why risk the future?'

'You're off your carrot,' the girl said. 'They've been shooting each other down like ninepins already!'

Louis started away from the truck.

'Is that why you said Ferdi might be dead?' he cried.

'I don't know if he is or not,' I said.

'Hey!' Pommie said, with sudden urgency. 'Look at this!' He beckoned with a wildly waving arm. 'They're going to come up here!'

'Open the gates!' the girl said, and ran to the machinery.

'They're coming right on up,' Pommie said. 'They got guns. It's a long climb yet, but they're coming!'

Louis darted to the back of the truck, bent and snatched up the automatic rifle. I saw him tugging at it, trying to make it click. 'It will not work!' he gasped. 'You have wrecked it!'

'There's four lots of guns down there,' Pommie said, hoarsely. 'How many we got?'

'Two,' I said, 'and five loose bullets with a full magazine. That's eleven, plus — ' I snapped out the Mauser's magazine. 'Plus nothing,' I said, and tossed the gun away on the grass.

'Will not the bullets fit?' Louis said.

'I have only thirty-eight bullets. They won't fit the Mauser. I'm afraid we'll have to let the water out. Perhaps they can swim.'

219

'It won't shift!' the girl panted, shoving and tugging at the big handle. 'It won't turn. That damn bolt has jammed the whole lot!'

10

The Germans were coming up the slope, spread out like a trained army. Which they were. The Movement was an organisation which kept them fully employed by teaching various arts which one day might come in handy.

Their line was staggered, so that one behind covered two ahead. There were seven men all coming silently up the slope towards us, their Lugers held at the ready.

Pommie and I crouched at the edge, peering over. The girl struggled with the gate machinery, panting, gasping, getting nowhere for the crunched bolt was stuck in the gear teeth.

Louis held the useless automatic rifle. After all, the oncomers didn't know it wouldn't fire.

'They will leave no one alive,' he said. 'It is an easy place to hide bodies and keep secrets.'

Well, one had been kept for almost a quarter of a century in these hills, and only the approaching death of the one man who knew of it had revealed it now. Nobody came up here any more.

Nobody would be here now if it hadn't been for the greed of adventurers. They were killing each other, yet there was enough to share out.

One of the Germans saw Pommie's head and fired. Two more fired, crossfire to discourage us from replying. The leading men began to run, but it was heavy going up the slope.

They fired more. It was a barrage, meant to keep us back while they got up and over the lip of the embankment.

Pommie went right back. Until that time I had held from the flooding principle because the oncomers hadn't done anything to persuade me they meant nasty business. The burst of firing now left no further doubt. Louis was right.

Though I had myself seen the Jerries firing at Ferdi and company, they had been returning fire. This time they didn't mean to leave any to return.

222

I went over to the struggling girl at the machine.

'You're doing it the wrong way. Let go.'

She let the handle go and fell back, panting with the effort.

I got hold of the old iron crank and wound it back. The rusty teeth pushed the bolt free.

'Pick it out!' I said, holding the weight hard against my chest. The handle was trying to turn on its own, the weight of the water on the gates shoving back through the gears with more force than I had expected.

She bent in and got the bolt out. I let go and jumped back.

The big handle spun round and round and the rusty teeth screamed in grinding freedom. But it was a sound soon drowned by the cracking of the gates and the devastating roar of the released torrent.

There were wild shouts from beyond the edge of the drop. I ran to it and looked down upon the seven men, all still as tin soldiers, looking at the flood bursting down on them like some furious

223

monster wild for destruction.

Then they began to move. They turned, started to run down the slope, tripping and stumbling from sheer speed on the gradient.

But the water was faster. We saw the great wave of frothing green burst down upon the running men. We saw them vanish, then appear on the boiling surface like corks bouncing on the flood. They were carried down, sometimes going under the torrent, sometimes half-standing up out of it, then being swept on down, toys in the flood.

The water reached the working floor and hurled itself at the old wooden buildings. One after another they were pushed over, bursting like matchboxes as they went, rolling as they disintegrated.

The men were still visible now and again, but the water hit the far rock wall of the floor, burst up it like a great explosion, then fell back on its following body.

It was like a maelstrom, spinning, fighting itself, hurling the wreckage it had made into the air in bursts of spray.

Louis the tough was muttering a prayer by my side, but I found it was a plea for forgiveness, not a call for mercy for the drowning men.

He must have almost shouted it, for the roaring of the water was like thunder on the air.

The girl stood by me and I saw her face. I could see she had never properly imagined what this flood was going to be like.

The whole of the working floor was now a frothing mass of seething water, with wreckage spinning, jumping out and falling back in. Men, too.

But the outlet to the workings began to take some of the dreadful volume of water away. The flood eased in its fury as the relief valves of the tunnels began to have their effect.

'That's an Acter God, that is,' Pommie said, wiping his face. 'A damn Acter God. They'd have wiped out the lot of us.'

The girl turned her back on it and watched the slow emptying of the lake.

'Are there any more of them?' Louis said.

'There could be,' I said. 'They looked as if they didn't mean to lose. Perhaps they started out with that idea. If so there could be more.'

'They're going into the workings like fleas down a sink,' Pommie said, with relish.

The girl walked over to the lake shore, now a steep run down to the sinking level of the water. I could see her pretty little mind was still fixed on getting that loot. It made me feel very tired, not to say sick.

All through I had been unable to understand her greedy attitude. I had tried to excuse it by substituting high spirits, adventurousness, love of kicks, but in my heart I knew she was hooked on that treasure, and that even at this late stage, she hadn't changed.

How the hell my friend's daughter could have got such a sordid greed in her soul I didn't know, but then, I didn't know her anyway. We had met at parties at his home, parties where she had been as greedy for notoriety as she was now for loot.

She had had to be the one to paint her

face green and stick small diamonds all round her eyes, or slant almond eyes deep painted on her own with metal hats and ear-rings.

'This is my daughter! You've met her!' he had said and laughed.

Then again, 'Don't you know me?' At that time she had been done up as a Chinese pagoda. Some other time she had been painted black with silver eyelids and lips and posed as a negative.

It got in the papers all right. As I looked at her then, with torn shirt and riding breeches, with dusty boots and dirty face, I realised this was the one and only time she would try to keep out of the papers.

That I should be thinking of parties back in London, where there was nothing more dangerous than a flirt or a drink, was a sign I was getting very tired indeed.

In fact, the roaring of the water became almost a lullaby. I sat on the grass, hugged my knees and tried to think seriously of what was to be done now.

I had a feeling, it could have been the depression that comes with exhaustion, that there were more Krauts down below, and that the truck was too big not to be noticed even from a long distance.

If we had known what had been the outcome of the cave battle it wouldn't have helped. For unless both sides had died at the same instant, like Abdul and Ivan, there was one enemy left.

'Are there just the four of you?' I called up to Louis.

'There were six,' he said, with a curious smile. 'You shot two. Up there.'

'They tried to burn us alive,' I reminded him

He shrugged.

The girl did not move from watching the water going slowly down the retaining walls of the lake. Across, teetering, almost, on the other side the great heaped pile of stones seemed to be leaning over, watching the water as she was.

'There are just four of us,' Louis said, squatting on his haunches by my side. 'Why should we not make a business arrangement? Not to make one is sure to mean somebody else getting killed.'

'All I want is to get out of here,' I said.

'I don't believe you are as crazy as that,' he said. 'If you say correct, when the water is gone, the — collection will be easily reached. All we have to do is wait.'

'Suppose there are more Krauts about? We shan't have any water next time.'

'We can blow them up,' he said, looking thoughtfully at the truck.

'You exaggerate,' I said. 'What are you going to do, sling bits of jelly at them?'

'Pommie knows,' he said confidently.

I encouraged him to go on talking while I tried to think how I could get the girl out of this place. It was a good long walk back on this track to the village round the hill, but once there what?

We had had enough of the road down, and we had no car. We had no sort of vehicle, for we wouldn't be able to get my car up over that four foot drop as easily as she had dropped down it.

We had no sort of vehicle.

Except the truck.

I was beginning to wake up. The downswing after the water stopped action had reached bottom and was returning.

★ ★ ★

The girl came back to me. She looked soft and innocent and I was immediately watchful.

'It will soon be empty,' she said.

'And the lootshop will be full,' I said.

'Look, it's silly to go now,' she said reasonably. 'It's all there. Practically staring you in the face. Millions. Why are you so against it? It doesn't belong to anybody.'

I looked at Louis, standing up now and looking out over the dwindling lake.

'I've explained it all before,' I said. 'Why go on? It's worth millions. It's useless. For God's sake have some sense.'

Then she got sly again.

'Well, I mean, we're not going to walk, are we? And we haven't got a motor. So why not do something interesting?'

I was thinking, All I have to do is whack her over the head with the gun, hold the other two up and pinch the truck.

But it seemed too easy.

'Pommie,' I said as he came up to go to

the truck cab, 'what cargo have you got?'

He laughed.

'A new disturber,' he said. 'Enough to shake the whole of these mountains to little dirty bits.'

'Is it touchy?'

'Touchy enough. You don't want to shake it up too much or it'll shake you. Some blowers are nervous of it. No good being nervous. That makes you shaky. Then you might drop something.'

All four of us now were watching the lake empty. The water looked almost down to the mud, but it was still rushing strongly through the open gateway.

I looked up towards the moon and saw someone moving over in a batch of trees across the lake. I didn't say anything. It might be better to save it for a surprise.

The person had come from somewhere near the rock pile and I had just got a glimpse of him as he ducked into the cover of the trees. One man.

It wouldn't be a Kraut, I thought. They moved in battalions, never less than three.

The one man most likely to be on his own was Ferdi. But if it was, why hide from his own truck, his own men?

Ferdi had nothing to fear. He had the major bargaining weapon, the disposal line.

Yet he had made that odd offer to get me in with them. Suddenly I wondered if he had meant for me to side with him in case of trouble with his henchmen.

But why should he have trouble when they were so dependent on him?

Then I remembered his story of how his girl secretary had snatched the map from the copier.

Why risk making a copy of such a precious map as that one? It was a case of the fewer the safer. And he had left it in the copier and gone to answer the phone!

How in hell I could have been so pressed to get out of the place that I hadn't bothered to test that one beat me then. But all through, I hadn't bothered with anything save getting myself and the girl out of this ferocious mountain.

Since that time I hadn't more than a few odd minutes to spare to think of it, but once started, I went on.

Here was a truckload of high explosive,

a highly dangerous cargo, sensitive to shaking. Hence the very low speed the truck had always used.

But why a truckload? An experienced explosive man like Pommie could have met any old mine with a few sticks of normal combustible material. Why a truckload?

Also I had seen no indication on the map that any blowings would be necessary. Falls in the years might have made blowing necessary, but Ferdi had never been to this place before.

If he had, he wouldn't have wasted time chasing us up to the village. He could have left a couple of men to keep us quiet and then got into the workings.

But he had followed the girl.

Then, when he thought we were hiding in the quarry, he had not sent Louis or Pommie or Digger but had come himself.

This little man, who had a nervous thing about the dark, had come himself without any of his men covering him as they had up in the village street.

Then he had gone off on his own into the dark without a light.

And then the idea occurred to me that he might have expected to find somebody in the quarry that he knew. That could have been why he had come alone, why he had risked going into the dark alone.

But why leave his henchmen and come into a dangerous place alone? Except to meet someone he expected.

And why should a man who had stood in the street facing my possible bullets be so nervous of the dark in the tunnels?

Could it have been that having met the person he didn't want to meet, he was scared of meeting the one that he did in my company?

Had he known someone — not me — should be ahead of him in the dark?

The whole picture began to change. The apparent motive of the great treasure was not so clear now. Something else, some vague supposition, was coming in front of it.

Were all the chalk swastikaed bosoms filled with diamonds? Or were there just a few? Just three. Just enough to fill her pockets?

Were the wild paintings really covering

rare oils beneath?

I had to think I was wrong then, for the girl was so mad to get back there that she couldn't know there wasn't any more to get her greedy little hands on.

As I changed my mind on these ponderings I made it up on another matter.

'There's a man hiding over in the trees,' I said.

Both Louis and Pommie looked up sharply. Very sharply.

The girl however, looked as sharply — at me.

'Where?' Pommie said hoarsely.

'In that clump. Take your gun and creep up on him. You can do it now, in the shore of the lake that wasn't there before.'

Pommie kept staring and muttered something. Louis glanced at me.

'You would not be mistaken?' he said.

'Why?'

He shrugged and accepted that there could be no reason why I would say there was a man if there wasn't.

'Come on,' Pommie said to him. 'Bring that gun.'

'I'll cover you,' I said.

I remained sitting while they went over the edge of the lake and down the steep decline towards the water, then I got up.

'What are you up to?' the girl said.

'Get in the truck,' I said quietly, and as she hesitated, 'I'll blow your head off if you don't!'

'You can't say that to me — '

'Get in the truck. If it helps, I know what you're up to. Now get in that cab!'

She watched me a moment, wiping her hands down her thighs, then she turned and got up into the cab.

The two men were walking slowly along the deepest part of the shore. The water was so low now that I could see the queer looking black spots which must be the upward windows of the loot cavern.

One looked back and when he saw me standing at the front of the truck he seemed satisfied and went on.

The man who had gone into the trees had made no other move. The two men on the lake bed — for it was almost that now — split up. Pommie went prowling ahead, past the point where the trees stood above him. Louis stopped short.

They were going to come up on the hider from two sides, and their movement was smooth and practised. They had clearly worked together before.

They started to go up the slope, like flies crawling up a wall.

I got up into the truck.

'You won't get away,' she said.

'I can always try. How many men do you think are dead, due to you?'

She said nothing.

'Well, this one isn't going to add to the others.'

I started the engine. The descending roar of the waters still sluicing through the gates covered the engine noise. We backed round slowly, so that no sudden movement might be caught from the eye corner of one of the climbing men.

They were almost at the top when I headed down the track and crumped the gears into bottom.

I didn't hear the gun firing, just saw a series of flashes from in amongst the trees. Something hit the bonnet, then the cab behind my head, then we heard plops

237

from somewhere in the back.

At almost that moment, Louis and Pommie ran in amongst the trees and the firing stopped.

'He's hit the jelly!' she said, struggling suddenly. 'Let me get out!'

In the mirror at the side of the cab I could see the tarpaulin cover smoking. I held her still with one hand locking her wrist and kept on driving.

The back of the cab was open and looking back I saw a lot of boxes piled in the wagon, rocking slightly with the bumping along the old track.

And as I looked a tongue of flame shot up the tarpaulin hood on the inside.

'Get out!' she screamed.

'Get in the back and beat that out. There's a lot of sacks lying there. Flog it! Go on! I'm not stopping. Don't try and jump. I'm going fast.'

She gasped, and as I let her go I saw her look to the window to judge the speed. It was too fast. She clambered over into the back, picked up a sack and started to flog the burning tarpaulin.

Smoke and sparks scattered around the

crates and I heard her panting with her desperate efforts to beat the flame out.

Gradually the burning streak of canvas turned into choking smoke and I heard her coughing with it. I could see her in the centre mirror as she fell back, thinking her job done.

But as she did, the flame flared up anew. She started to beat furiously, but this time the sacking she used seemed to spread it.

Then I saw the sack itself catch fire.

We were going pretty fast down the track then, heading for the curve that went round the hill. By the look of the rate the fire was now spreading we wouldn't even reach the bend.

'I can't! I can't!' she screamed.

I hauled on the brake. The vehicle slid round on the grass and almost heeled over. I had the door open before she stopped and dropped to the ground.

The tarpaulin was ablaze all along the side now as I ran beside it to the tail. She was at the tail-board, one foot over it, apparently paralysed with fear.

'Jump!' I shouted.

I heard her whimper and then gasp as she tried to clamber over the board. But she was so panicky she just let go and fell over head first.

Before she actually hit the ground I got her and started to run towards the lake, carrying her with her legs round my neck, her arms gripping my waist.

At the edge of the decline I just jumped, lost my footing and, still locked together like two lobsters in mortal combat, we rolled over and over down the slippery lake shore to the bottom and into three inches of water.

That was all that was now left of the thousands of tons we had started with.

We untangled, rolling in the mud, fighting to get up on the slippery bottom.

Then it came. An almost gentle roar at first, growing slowly until it filled the ears with pain and the ground shook as it had in the avalanches.

A great pillar of white flame shot into the sky from beyond the rim of the lakeside, growing into orange and red with bits of the truck flying upwards in its heavenly ascent. Smoke piled up above it, billowing away like great cumulus clouds in the moonlight.

The column rose higher and higher, beyond the mountain peaks, high into the sky, rolling, billowing, spreading.

Then the flame ran back down to the ground again and there was left only a last tongue of orange fire, licking lazily into the smoke mass.

'A good thing we missed that,' I said, and got some of the lake water in my hands and drank it, muddy as it was.

She just lay in the water, half-curled, leaning on one arm, covered in mud from head to foot. She looked like a seal.

I looked up across the lake to where Louis and Pommie had gone.

'My God! Look at that!' I shouted.

The great pile of mighty stones was tottering now, swaying, like a concertinaed backbone. How long it had stood there, balancing against the storms and tempests of the years I do not know, but the load in that lorry proved better than Nature.

It rocked enough, stayed suspended, leaning over the lake bed, and then it toppled. The giant size of the stones made the fall look like slow motion as they came, parting from each other, falling outwards.

Then they began to hit the lake bed, crashing, thundering quite softly after the ear-burning roar of the explosion. But the lake bed began to give. One or two stones crashed through the false roof of the loot cavern and disappeared within. Others came on top and gradually piled up, spreading out making a mighty impassable plug to the hole in the lootshop roof.

'Oh no!' she said. 'Oh no!'

The great fall ended, mighty discs of stone lying about the lake floor round the centre under which the rich cavern had been.

'Now you'll have to blow it really up this time,' I said. 'Except that your truck wasn't meant to blow up stone, was it?'

'It wasn't my truck. It was theirs,' she said angrily.

'But the jelly was intended to blow up the Movement expeditionary force, wasn't it? Isn't the whole thing political? Where was Ferdi's outlet for the stuff? I thought all along of the wicked millionaires of Texas and places West. But now I think the outlet was to be in the East. Would you admit that?'

She didn't say anything.

'The treasure is here, perhaps. All that story of the horde brought to this mountain by Gleist, may well be true. But Ferdi's idea was to use it as a trap to wipe out the whole branch of The Movement which has been secretly training in Spain. Would you say that is so?

'The stories about Ferdi's secretary — your friend who sold you the map and the gun are all a lot of lies. All that happened was that at the last moment you, having got your silly self involved in Ferdi's anti *drang nach Osten*, lost your nerve, took the map and bolted.

'And that was where I came in.'

'I didn't have any political sympathies — not that strong, anyhow,' she said bitterly. 'I got involved in a peace movement, and Ferdi was on the end and I started telling a lot of lies of what I'd done in England and New York, and all sorts of things and he believed them and

243

that's how it happened.'

'And once you were on the inside and got the drift about the map trap, you thought of all this wealth lying around, just going East and being squandered on political affairs when it could do you worlds of good. So you nicked the map and ran.

'Ferdi wasn't ready, was he? But he had to follow. So you then played a very dangerous game of tipping off the Germans in the hope they would meet with Ferdi and the battle take place while you snitched a small fortune and hopped it. Do I have it aright?'

'You have it aright. But I did ring from the hotel vestibule to the Jerries before I had to make the run.'

'Is that why you went off alone into the dark?'

'To meet the leader. Yes.'

'Up in the village, Ferdi appeared to want to blow you apart. Down in the quarry he soft-shoed in by himself. So up there he was putting on a face to persuade his helpers he wouldn't make a deal with you?'

'Well, his men had no political affiliations. They were a gang of assorted back-trackers wanted by jails in several countries. They were brought in for a share of the loot. It's the only way to get them.'

'So that the big bang theory would have disintegrated them as well as the Movement?'

She sat up in the mud then.

'You can't trust Ferdi,' she said blandly.

'So that in fact what Ferdi could have meant to do was to destroy the Nazi movement and what was apparently his own left movement?'

She laughed then and wiped mud from her face.

'You could be right,' she said.

'It would account for the fact that he acted like two different men on different occasions.'

'Agents have to — ' There she stopped, and to cover the slip, got up out of the mud. 'We must get out of here now. The police will come to see what the explosion was. It must have been seen down in the town.'

She sounded calm, unlike the wild one that had led me such a dance through that day.

'You seem almost a different person, too,' I said.

I thought she laughed as we sloshed across the lake bed towards the spot where we had last seen Pommie and Louis go in.

Under the trees there was only Ferdi. The other two, no doubt thinking with the girl that the cops would soon be here, had gone.

Ferdi wasn't dead, but he looked as if he had fallen out with his one time helpers, for he had his eyes closed and breathed very hard as he lay there, knocked out.

'Leave him,' she said.

We went on down towards the valley where I had seen a way up over the hills, betting on the cops coming in at the front entrance, or down the track from the village.

'It occurs to me,' I said as we walked fast, 'that as we stand now, the two movements have been badly disrupted

246

and the agent for the East is also put out. That is three parties with their tricks confounded. And you walk out alone.'

She walked on.

'So wanting to go back to the loot wasn't for the loot, but to check up on where everybody was and make sure their tricks would cancel out each other? Not for sordid gain?'

She smacked her pockets and walked on.

'An agent, you say he was — ' I said.

'They're not so rare,' she said. 'But you're forgetting your duty.'

'My duty?'

'You promised to get me home to Daddy.'

'What — again?' I sighed.

THE END

THE MAYHEM MADCHEN
THE DEATH IMPORTER
THE THUG EXECUTIVE
A WREATH OF BONES
THE CASE OF THE FEAR MAKERS
A FALL-OUT OF THIEVES
THE FARM VILLAINS

We do hope that you have enjoyed reading this large print book.

Did you know that all of our titles are available for purchase?

We publish a wide range of high quality large print books including:
**Romances, Mysteries, Classics
General Fiction
Non Fiction and Westerns**

Special interest titles available in large print are:
**The Little Oxford Dictionary
Music Book, Song Book
Hymn Book, Service Book**

Also available from us courtesy of Oxford University Press:
**Young Readers' Dictionary
(large print edition)
Young Readers' Thesaurus
(large print edition)**

For further information or a free brochure, please contact us at:
**Ulverscroft Large Print Books Ltd.,
The Green, Bradgate Road, Anstey,
Leicester, LE7 7FU, England.
Tel:** (00 44) **0116 236 4325
Fax:** (00 44) **0116 234 0205**